ALSO BY GW

SECRETS IN THE BLOOD

GWYN BENNETT

Storm

To request permissions, contact the publisher at rights@stormpublishing.co

Ebook ISBN: 978-1-80508-309-2
Paperback ISBN: 978-1-80508-311-5

Cover design: Eileen Carey
Cover images: Shutterstock

Published by Storm Publishing.
For further information, visit:
www.stormpublishing.co

PROLOGUE
WEDNESDAY

His fear smelt of damp and urine. Acidic champagne bile forced its way up into his throat and mouth, burning the back of his tongue. One minute it had been a celebration, a triumph. The next he was pleading for his life.

There was nothing but the sound of anger ricocheting off the concrete walls. He understood the feeling of betrayal. He couldn't deny them that.

His brain was slow. Tiredness and alcohol dumbing down his processing despite the adrenaline, but he listened in the darkness, and he tried to talk them out of killing him.

He'd no idea how long it had been, but at some point, a strange calmness had come over him. He'd tried everything. Arguing back. Reasoning. Pleading. He'd even sobbed and promised to make things right, but eventually he'd known there was no going back. He would have to pay the price.

He bowed his head, all hope leaching from his body and blending with the wet that had seeped through the knees of his trousers. The stench of damp and urine no longer registering. In the pitch-black darkness, he saw the faces of his family. He imagined their reactions to the news of his death. The last thing in his head before the bullet ripped through it, was what the headline about his murder might be in the *Jersey Evening Post*.

ONE

THURSDAY

'Look at that view, isn't it just beautiful?' Doug Miller put out his hand to help his wife, Nancy, from the hire car, but his eyes were focused across the cliff top to Portelet Bay.

She huffed and groaned as she stood up.

'We really should have got the bigger car,' she said to Doug as she straightened out her aching back and legs.

'What? Around those tiny lanes they have here? Did you want to lose the auto insurance excess?'

Nancy didn't reply, but instead turned her eyes to where Doug was looking.

'That's another of those old Napoleonic towers, isn't it?' she said, squinting in the already bright sunshine despite the early hour. In front of them, across the gorse bushes and below the perfect blue sky, was a small bay with golden sand and aquamarine sea. In the middle of the horseshoe-shaped cove was a tiny island with a squat granite tower on top.

'Looks that way,' he replied. 'Not sure how we get down there.'

'We don't. Least not this morning. My knees won't take much more walking and climbing down cliff tops,' Nancy replied, looking around for the reason they'd driven to this spot. 'Anyways, let's take a look here first.'

Nancy and Doug Miller were retirees from Pennsylvania. In their late sixties, they were midway through their big European tour, taking in some of the locations that Doug's father had talked about visiting while in the US navy during the Second World War; as well as a few bucket list places that Nancy had always dreamt about. They'd walked the length and breadth of Venice, Paris, Rome, and Athens. Now, en route to London, they'd stopped off in Jersey, the largest of the British Channel Islands, just off the French coast.

'Watch where you're treading,' Doug warned his wife, offering his arm. 'There are lots of loose stones.'

'What's that?' They'd come up to some metal structures, one a round block sticking up out of a concrete bunker with a thick metal pole going through its middle, and the others, two metal domes. This was Batterie Lothringen, one of the fortifications built in the island by the occupying German forces during the Second World War.

'That's the range finder,' Doug said, consulting his guidebook and pointing to the first structure with the arms. 'And those are observation cupolas. Just take a look at that view they'd have had. Not surprising they chose to build here. They'd have seen anything coming for miles.' The pair of them stood and just looked for a few moments. 'Somewhere here is the memorial to the US Navy PT boat squadron that my dad was part of. They lost some men when they attacked a German convoy taking armaments between the Channel Islands,' Doug added, turning away from the sea to concentrate back on land.

The couple walked a little further, and came to the other side of the narrow headland that looked out across St Aubin's Bay with St Helier in the distance. Doug stopped, taking some time to think about his father and the men who had died.

'It wasn't the Germans who built all this though, was it? Those poor slave workers did.' Nancy had a Polish grandparent and she'd already got upset the day before at the memorial to the forced workers at La Houge Bie. Now, she brushed her hands across the soft heads of the hare's tail grasses which were growing against the granite wall beside her, finding comfort in their touch. 'It doesn't look much...' she ventured, looking at the metal structures.

'It's like an iceberg, Nancy. We're standing on top of a huge tower, it's got five floors would you believe?' Doug waved the guidebook in her direction.

Behind them, another couple of cars had joined theirs in the car park, slowly scrunching to a halt in the dusty gravel. The spot was a regular for tourists and dog walkers. The Millers had been first to arrive, up early, keen to maximise their sightseeing for what was only a short trip to the island. Having looked at the size of Jersey when they were planning their trip, they hadn't expected to need long to cover the nine-by-five miles island, the whole place smaller than Pittsburgh; but had been surprised by just how much there was to see.

Twenty minutes later, the sun was starting to climb, and Nancy was feeling the heat. They'd walked past a giant gun which they'd read was No. 2 gun, and read a blue plaque which talked about the naval battle off the point on the 9th August 1944 and pointed to the memorial that Doug had wanted to find. They then came to a concrete slope that led downwards, with metal safety railings all around the top.

'I'm going to look down here,' Nancy said to her husband who had stopped to inspect the mustard-yellow lichen on the granite wall next to some steps. He was a retired microbiologist with more than a passing interest in lichenology.

Nancy walked down the slope, feeling the warmth of the sun on the top of her head. On her right was an open passageway which led inside to what she presumed would have been bunkers. There was a rusting metal frame on the door with hinges that had once held a door.

'I'm just going inside here,' she called out to Doug as she stepped up into the bunker, looking forward to some cool air. 'You coming?'

The interior was dark, just a scrap of light coming down from the ceiling further inside. Other than that, it was only the shaft of sun from the doorway that gave any illumination, and so Nancy had pulled her mobile phone from her pocket and turned on the torch. All of this section was built from light-grey concrete slabs. It wasn't a large area; there were two entrances leading off on the right, both again missing their actual doors. She struggled to see inside the first, a stench of urine and damp hitting her nostrils as she peered into the gloom, making her stay on the threshold. This place had clearly been used by some visitors as a toilet. Disgusting. Her nose wrinkled up and she instinctively brought her sleeve up to try to smother the stench, stepping back into the corridor and the fresher air.

The whole place made her skin creep. She imagined the ghosts of the many slave workers who'd died building the concrete fortifications. Were their bodies buried in the structures, like some believed? Did their tortured souls seep out of the concrete like the white salt moisture crystals?

Nancy called out to Doug again, 'Dougie, you coming? I'm inside this bunker.'

He didn't reply and she nearly walked back out, but they'd come a long way to visit this place and she wanted to make the most of it. They needed photos to show the folks back home, and besides Dougie would only say that her imagination was working overtime again.

She paused again on the threshold of the concrete room, and took a couple of shots, the flash from her phone camera illuminating the walls. On the right side wall a white chalked or spray-painted swastika appeared out of the darkness, the initials

AH above it. 'Kids,' she muttered to herself, shaking her head at their lack of respect. She took another photograph over towards the left, hoping it wouldn't show anything disgusting, as suggested by the smell. She was interested to see how far the room went back and if there was anything inside it. She was wondering if this might be where ammunition was stored for the big gun they'd just looked at.

Nancy waited for the picture to take, the camera aperture working hard to create an image in the darkness. Finally she drew her hand back and looked at what it had captured, expecting to see more graffiti. Instead, the concrete wall was splattered in red, drips of it running down the walls, and there was a humped shape on the floor. It took only a second for Nancy to realise that the humped shape was a man, slumped forward on his knees.

Nancy's heart exploded in a white hot jolt of fear. Her throat instantly closed up and she nearly dropped her phone as she stumbled backwards into the concrete wall behind her, staring at the black doorway in front. Nothing moved. Nothing came at her out of the darkness. There was no breathing. No sound. No sound until the scream began to rise up in Nancy's throat, a high-pitched gurgling at first, before it forced its way past the knots of fear that held her body rigid, and came out of her mouth like a high-pitched air raid klaxon.

TWO

THURSDAY

'Why do you get to say what's the right or wrong way to react? Who made you God?'

Gary Lewis stared at Saskia's colleague, challenging him to reply.

'Yeah. Why am I always the bad one? Maybe youse people don't understand me.' Carlos Rodriguez was fired up by Gary's support.

There were seven of them, all sitting in a circle for a group therapy session at La Moye prison. Forensic psychologist Saskia Monet and her colleague had their backs to the door in order to ensure that the five prisoners couldn't get between them and the exit. From what had been a relaxed start to the session, the atmosphere had quickly developed into a prickly static. Group therapy was a standard rehabilitation treatment within prisons, but Saskia hadn't been involved in the choice of participants for this group and it was clear that one man was dominating the room.

'You wanted to be included in the group,' Edward, the facilitator, tried to reason with Carlos, ignoring Gary's interruption.

'He only did it to tick one of your boxes for early release. I don't want to be here either. I don't see the point of any of this. What are you actually trying to achieve here?' Gary took over again and Carlos was happy to let him lead. 'I mean, what do we get out of sitting around in a circle raking over what happened according to whatever the police made up to get their false convictions? What scientific evidence is there to say that this helps anybody?'

Gary Lewis, known as the mermaid killer, had been at La Moye for only a short while before Saskia had joined. She'd not yet fully assessed him and his behaviour now meant that he would be going to the top of her list. The psychologist investigator who'd helped catch him, Dr Harrison Lane from the Ritualistic Behavioural Crime unit in the UK, had intimated that he believed him to be a psychopath and yet it appeared that nobody had run any tests on Gary, perhaps because he was a reluctant participant.

Saskia agreed wholeheartedly with Harrison Lane. Gary had clear psychopathic traits which would make him totally unsuited to group work. Psychopaths were often disruptive in programmes like this. Group therapy only helped if you wanted to change, which of course they didn't because they didn't think there was anything wrong with their behaviour. They also served as training grounds for them, letting psychopaths observe people under emotional stress, often finding new ways to manipulate and emulate them.

'I think we've all had enough for today,' she said to them, closing up her notebook to show she meant it. 'It's nearly time for lunch, so let's get you all back to your cells.'

'Can't take it when the questions get turned on you, Miss Monet?' Gary Lewis said to her snidely, emphasising the 'miss'. 'Getting too hot for you is it with all this testosterone?'

'No, Gary. It's lunchtime and you need to go and collect your food so that you can be locked safely away in your cell to eat it. You wouldn't want to miss out, now would you?'

He'd been trying to be domineering, but she'd countered his sexist jibes by emphasising the fact he would be locked away again while she did what she wanted.

Once the prisoners had all been escorted away, she spoke to Edward.

'Who agreed to putting Gary Lewis into group therapy?'

'I think it was actually his suggestion. He'd seemed like he wanted to participate.'

'Yeah well, he's an intelligent man and he gets bored in here. He's just using it as a way to manipulate other vulnerable prisoners for his own amusement. I'm certain he'd score highly on the PCL-R test as a high-functioning psychopath. I'll put him down for a full assessment and see what we can do with him, but he needs to be restricted from taking advantage of vulnerable prisoners.'

Edward nodded. 'What do you think about the others?'

'I'd give it a break for a couple of weeks and then try again. They may still be receptive once he's out the equation. Have you got another prisoner who's been through the programme and found it useful? If you can add him in instead, then it might encourage the others.'

'Thanks,' Edward replied. Saskia got the impression he was a little out of his depth with some of the prisoners who were more manipulative like Gary. Just the thought that somebody was a psychopath could terrify people. Not her, though. A childhood surviving a psychopathic father and a lifetime of trying to keep David, her brother, on the straight and narrow, had given her more than enough experience to handle the best of them. Perhaps she could get Edward to sit in on the assessment with Gary so he'd be able to watch and learn how she dealt with him.

Saskia headed to her own office for lunch and to attend to her no doubt full email inbox. On the way, she had the misfortune of having to pass Mark Byrne, the other likely psychopath in the prison – only he was on the wrong side of the fence. The big, bearded prison guard was her least favourite person at La Moye, even after the inmates. He had taken an instant dislike to Saskia, possibly just out of contempt for her profession, or possibly because he realised she recognised him for what he was. Mark stared at her as they approached each other in the corridor and it was only the opportune arrival of another colleague that meant he didn't barge straight into her, swerving at the last second. She ignored him. Not rising to his intimidation was her best retaliation, but he did worry her. She'd no idea what he was capable of.

Saskia had brought her own packed lunch in as usual and settled down at her desk to eat it. Most of the staff did, very few of them wanting to get food from the prison canteen. She'd made herself a nice Greek tomato salad along with some leftover chicken that she'd cooked last night. This morning she'd had to wrestle with Bilbo and his big 'feed me' eyes to get any of the leftovers, but she'd managed to be strong enough to give him a share that kept him happy and some for her own lunch.

She thought about her big fat cat sitting on his windowsill in the sun snoozing with a nice full belly. She'd bought him his own cushion for the windowsill so it was a softer, more comfortable perch for the day. There'd been no thanks, just a dismissive flick of his tail before he curled up and closed his eyes. He had a tough life.

She'd just finished her last mouthful of salad and chicken, when her mobile rang and Detective Inspector Winter Labey's name flashed up. Her stomach did a little flip of excitement – definitely not a common occurrence. Was that because she'd missed speaking to him, or because she'd missed the excitement of being a part of a live case? After helping him with profiling on the Pied Piper investigation, he'd said he might call her again if they ever needed her.

'DI Labey,' she said as she answered the call.

'Miss Monet,' he replied. Both of them taking a slightly joking tone with the formal titles. They'd long since started calling each other Winter and Saskia.

'What can I do for you?' she asked, enjoying the sound of his voice. It definitely had a manly tone, quite deep and just a little husky. She realised she was smiling.

'I'm sorry to call you at work, but we have a high-profile murder case that I would very much appreciate your opinions on.'

Saskia wasn't sure if she was a little disappointed that it was her professional opinion he was after, or not.

'Of course. I've not got any more appointments this afternoon if you need me now?'

'Well, I should warn you it's not a pretty sight. He's been shot in the head.'

'Right. Wish you'd called before my tomato salad,' Saskia replied. 'Seriously though, I'll be OK. I'm not squeamish.' It was true, there'd been more than a few injuries over the years that she'd had to deal with, not to mention some of the consequences of her brother's actions.

'If you're sure. We're at Noirmont, where the bunkers are on the headland. Are you familiar with it?'

'I haven't been since arriving in Jersey, but I'll find it. I'll leave now and should be with you within twenty minutes.'

'Thanks. I'll keep an eye out for you, just tell the officers on the cordon to radio me and they'll let you through.'

Saskia closed down her computer and got her motorbike helmet and backpack. If Winter needed her help then it was clearly not a straightforward homicide. She wondered what she was going to find at Noirmont Point and who the high-profile victim was.

THREE

David hadn't slept well for several nights. Not because he'd been stressed about anything or had aggravating insomnia like most people might experience, but because he'd been absolutely buzzing with excitement. It was such an unusual feeling for him that he quite simply hadn't known how to manage it. Jackie, his girlfriend, had returned home late on Sunday evening, tired and a little emotional after visiting her mother in a care home in England. When David had picked her up from the airport she'd been surprised that it was him and not her driver, Allan, in the arrivals hall.

'I wanted to meet you,' he'd said to her, giving her a sensual hug and kiss next to the stand of Jersey tourist leaflets advertising the various delights the island had to offer. She'd melted into him. 'Besides, he wasn't around. You didn't tell me he was having time off while you were away? I haven't seen him for a couple of days,' he'd said to her.

She'd pulled away from his embrace looking surprised and replied, 'He wasn't. If he's not been around then he's probably at Kevin's place. He knows you don't really need him and that I'm back tonight.' Later, as they were driving home, she'd added,

'It's unusual for Allan not to have been here for my flight back. He knew what time it was.'

She'd fallen into his trap just nicely.

'They had a big argument you know, him and Kevin. The night you left, a right old blow-up.'

'Really! And you haven't seen him since?' She was studying his profile – his handsome, chiselled profile – but he'd practised this exchange a hundred times over the weekend so he was ready.

'No. Oh, do you think I should have tried to contact him? Seen if he was alright? I just didn't think...' He left that hanging for her imagination.

'I'm sure he's fine.' She'd brushed it away and looked out the window. 'It's not like he doesn't know how to look after himself. The guy spent eight years in an English high-security prison. If he could survive that then he'll be fine in an argument with his boyfriend.'

'Really? I never knew he was an ex-con,' David casually replied. This was a new piece of information he might be able to use if required at a later time.

'Reformed, as you've seen. Nobody would give him a chance besides me, that's why he's so loyal.'

'What was he in for?' David enquired.

'Armed robbery,' Jackie answered. 'Anyway, what've you been up to while I've been away? Partying every night?'

David smiled, but not because of her question. Because Allan's past had fitted right into the little story he'd created to explain his disappearance. If only he could tell Saskia, she'd be so impressed with how he was covering his tracks.

'No,' he'd answered Jackie. 'What would I want to party without you for? I mostly hung about the house and went to the gym, had a quiet one.' Flashes of the last two days went through his mind. It had been the most exhilarating weekend of his life. He was simply fizzing inside. Was this how people felt when they were excited? Was this what made people scream on roller coasters and want to jump out of planes? Nothing else he'd ever done had created a feeling like this.

That night, once they'd got home from the airport, they'd eaten and then David had serviced Jackie, made her feel as though she was loved and missed. 'You know if there's ever anything I can do to help you with your mum, you must tell me,' he'd whispered to the top of her head, resting on his bare chest.

'Thank you, but it is what it is. I'm going to make sure I party hard so I die before I get too old.' She'd kissed his torso, running her hands over his tight abs. Not long after that, she'd fallen asleep.

David had listened to her breathing, thinking that perhaps, someday, he could help. A pillow over the old lady's face while she slept would do the trick.

Jackie had grown increasingly anxious about Allan over the following few days and they'd talked about reporting him as missing to the police. If he didn't contact her or turn up by tomorrow, Thursday, she was going to make the call. David encouraged her. He had nothing to fear.

Wednesday night, he'd lain in bed, his mind still bubbling with the weekend, re-living moments of it as his girlfriend softly snored beside him. He knew this euphoria wouldn't last long, but maybe if he kept replaying it in his head it would stay, become indelibly seared into his memory for him to savour whenever he wanted to. Every delicious second. He'd finally fallen asleep around three a.m., only to wake again at five-thirty. He'd crossed to the window and looked out at the garage block where Allan's flat was. There was no sign of activity or life. No Allan staring back at him. Watching. Of course there wasn't.

David couldn't face lying next to Jackie in bed again and so he'd gone downstairs and turned on the TV. Some inane cooking programme was on and he'd stared at the screen. It made him think of his father, although he doubted that his work as a chef had been anywhere near as fancy. It definitely wasn't now: he worked in the prison canteen, cooking slop for his fellow prisoners. For a split second, David thought about sharing the weekend with him. He'd understand… but then again, he'd also be more than happy to use it to his own advantage and tell the authorities to get some kind of privilege or to help his case for early release. That was never going to happen. He'd got two life sentences. A clear danger to society who would never be allowed back into it. No, David couldn't trust him. This would have to stay as his own secret.

The brainless television presenter was showing how to create a romantic breakfast, some trick to make a heart-shaped egg in a hole on toast. Jackie's alarm would be going off in half an hour – David wanted to keep her sweet and so he'd watched and learnt.

Half an hour later, as Jackie was woken by her alarm, David walked into their room carrying a tray of tea and heart-shaped eggs on toast.

'Wow!' she'd exclaimed. 'You really must have missed me.'

David gave her a kiss and went to the shower. He did his best thinking in the shower. With Allan out of the picture, he could now start putting the next stage of his plan into action. This house would be his within the year, and he wouldn't have to make heart-shaped eggs for anyone ever again.

FOUR

THURSDAY

The police cordon stretched down the road from Noirmont, to the small farm on the bend of Le Chemin de Noirmont and the turn off, which led on to Portelet Lane. Saskia had only been on the island a few months and she found the place a quaint mix of English and French-style buildings and rolling countryside. In one section there were continental-esque houses with verandas, in others, more traditional British architecture. She'd just passed the very English Marks & Spencer store opposite the fish and chip shop at Red Houses. Now, as she rode her motorbike down the lane to the point, past the granite farmhouse with its white-washed walls and blue-painted doors, she felt like she could be in France. The cluster of pines bordering the road and the dry, arid feel to the place with only gorse bushes and the occasional patch of green able to withstand the current hot sun and winds straight off the sea, reminded her of the coast in Bordeaux. She'd gone surfing around Montalivet between finishing school and starting university. The area had great waves coming straight off the Atlantic into the Bay of Biscay and for a few amazing weeks she'd been free.

It had been the only holiday she'd ever managed to take,

travelling around France and Italy in her beaten-up VW Golf in the days when the British had easy travel through Europe, thanks to being part of the EU. When she got back home, she'd had to clear up after one of David's 'episodes' as her mother called them back then. Another year later and her mother had left them both, unable to control Saskia's brother and in fear of her life. Saskia's university days hadn't been the carefree student experience of her peers.

This was her first visit to Noirmont Point, although she'd heard about it. She very much doubted her mother had ever brought her here as a child. Considering they left Jersey when she was just three, it was unlikely to be the sort of place you'd bring two very young children as it was surrounded by sheer rocky drops into the sea below. Especially when you had an eighteen-month old like her brother David who rarely did as he was told.

At the end of the road was a small car park which was currently filled with forensic and police vehicles. Saskia spotted Winter's tall, muscular frame; he was standing at the side of the parking area talking to one of the white-suited forensics officers who was just getting out of the coverall he was wearing. Winter raised a hand to her as she pulled in. The police officer on the cordon had already alerted him to her arrival.

'Thanks for coming at such short notice,' he said to her, appearing in front of her bike as she pulled off her helmet and shook out her long burnt-umber hair. 'And again, I apologise in advance for what you're about to see. If at any time you feel like you don't want to proceed, then please just say. One of the officers, who was a first responder, threw up so you'd be in good company.'

'Great, thanks, that makes me feel better,' Saskia replied, trying to make light of it. Winter was being protective. It was a trait she'd witnessed already in their short working relationship and while at times it could be unwanted, she did appreciate his gentle side. He was what some people might call a man's man – solid, fit and muscular but without being overly pumped. Unlike the carefully manicured style of her brother, Winter probably only looked in the mirror once a day, in the morning, to make sure his hair was combed and he was professionally presentable. He also seemed a little awkward around her – not so as people would notice, but Saskia did. She was trained to notice these things. Subtle changes in attitudes and demeanour of the prisoners she worked with could indicate danger to herself, others, or sometimes themselves. It meant she was finely tuned to the little nuances of someone's mannerism and personality and any changes in it. When she'd arrived, Winter had looked relaxed and at ease with the male forensics officer he'd been talking to. With her, he'd put on his kid gloves.

'Right, so: our victim is high profile, which has increased the pressure on the investigation from management, although in my view every victim deserves the same resources and effort,' Winter began. 'It's somewhat of an odd crime scene, which was why I've asked for your input. Not the usual crime of passion or professional hit. Right now, we have a totally open book on motive and killer identity so if you have any thoughts as to the kind of mind and person who did this, it would be gratefully received.'

'This place seems quite remote, how was he found?' Saskia asked. They'd started walking towards the crime scene.

'It seems like it's a bit out on a limb, but actually it's only a short walk from Portelet. There are a fair few houses across the fields down there, and this is a regular spot for both dog walkers and tourists who want to look at the bunkers. An American couple were here first this morning. The wife took a photograph inside a side room – it's usually pitch-black in there – and the image showed up our victim. It's only a small room. The main bunker and command post are locked. It's looked after by the Channel Island Occupation Society. They have regular open days when the whole place is opened up, but generally it's just what you see now plus a couple of small underground rooms.'

'So no idea of how long he'd been in there?'

'We do because we know who he is. His name's Paul Cabot and last night he was voted in as a deputy of the parish. His house is about a twenty-minute walk away. He hosted a small party there last night into the early hours. His wife went to bed at just gone one a.m. and she says he was still very much alive then.'

'So do you think it's politically motivated?' Saskia knew that the Jersey elections had taken place to elect representatives, called deputies, to the States of Jersey Assembly from which the government would be chosen.

'That's what Detective Chief Inspector Sharpe thinks,' Winter's tone changed at the mention of the DCI's name. They didn't exactly see eye-to-eye.

'But you don't agree?'

'I think he's putting United Kingdom political perspectives onto things here. Politics in Jersey are different. I'm not sure if you know, but we don't have fully formed party politics like in England – here, people stand on their own individual mani-festos, apart from the Reform Party. But even that isn't as struc-tured as the UK's parties are.'

'What kind of manifesto was Paul Cabot standing on?'

'Middle of the road. Nothing contentious. He was a popular choice. I've looked at what he was proposing and I can't see anything that's likely to encourage someone to want to kill him, although obviously we're going to need to dig a bit deeper and see if any extremists have taken umbrage at something he said.'

Saskia turned to study Winter's face. They'd come to a halt at the top of a concrete slope. Was the antagonism between him and the DCI making him look for an alternative motive just to be contrary, or was he being thorough? She decided on the latter.

'Anyway, I have an open mind,' Winter continued as if he'd read her thoughts. 'And now you'll see why the DCI has put two and two together to make five. Are you ready for this? It stinks in there, I'm afraid. Not just blood etc., but there's no toilets up here and Forensics don't think the stench of urine is just from our victim...' Winter hesitated. 'I err, I use some of this when I come across smells that are overpowering.' He pulled a small bottle from his pocket. 'Just rub a bit onto my wrist.'

He looked a little embarrassed and Saskia could tell that this was probably something he didn't share too often. She smiled softly at him.

'Thank you,' she said and offered up her thin wrist to his large hands.

'I can't remember what's in it, but I think it's lemon balm and stuff like that. All natural.'

He gently dabbed some of the oil onto her wrist and it glistened against her white skin and the blue threads of her veins. Winter held on to her wrist for perhaps a moment too long and she wondered if he was going to put more on. Then he let go. She rubbed the oil in with her other wrist and then brought it up to her nose.

'Nice.'

'This is between you and me though, right?' Winter said pocketing the little bottle again. 'Don't like to advertise it too much, I've got an image to maintain,' he said half-jokingly, as he walked down the slope ahead of her.

She smirked at his back and followed him.

At the bottom of the slope there was another cordon with a box of forensic overshoes and suits, and a police officer taking down the names of everyone who entered.

'You'll need to put this on,' Winter said, handing her a suit. 'That should be your size.'

She pulled the suit on and then the overboots, Winter doing the same next to her. They were at the entrance to an open-topped concrete tunnel, the concrete block walls about fifteen feet high. At the bottom of the gentle slope was an open doorway. Bright lights illuminated the interior and she could see someone else with a white suit, crouched down inspecting something on the floor.

'I'll let you go in first because there's not a lot of space in there,' Winter said. 'The victim is in the first room on the right. It's a slightly larger room than the other one, but we've no idea why that one was chosen except perhaps for convenience.'

Saskia nodded. Even before she entered the bunker, she could feel the atmosphere of the place. Whether it was the barren, disused state of it, or the story and history behind its existence, it made her skin crawl. Perhaps her long-forgotten animal instincts also smelt the death that awaited her inside. But Saskia was no stranger to danger and unpleasantness. She stepped over the threshold, ready for whatever lay beyond.

Immediately in front of her, at the end of the concrete corridor, was a red swastika graffitied onto the wall.

'Do you know if that's related?' She nodded to it, knowing Winter was right behind her.

'We don't believe so. We think that's kids, but it's being tested and we're checking with the Occupation Society.'

A few steps inside the doorway and there was another empty doorway to her right. This was filled with bright-white forensics lights. Saskia lifted her wrist to her nose and took a deep breath of Winter's scented oils, then stepped inside.

To her left was the body of a man dressed in a shirt and smart trousers. He was kneeling, slumped forward so that she couldn't see his head clearly. She quickly realised why that was, because some of his head had been splattered across the floor and wall in front of him.

Her wrist came up to her nose. The stench in here was as bad as Winter had warned her. High notes of stale urine combined with the rich undertone of iron-laden blood and freshly wounded flesh. There was no air supply circulating inside the concrete chamber, and the stench mixed with years of damp that crept out of the walls.

Saskia looked around the small room. There was nothing in there apart from the body and a white swastika on the right hand wall with the initials *AH* above it. She turned, having seen enough, and saw that Winter had already stepped out of the way of the doorway in case she needed a quick exit.

The second she stepped back out into the corridor, she caught the fresh air from outside and took some deep breaths.

'The forensic team have special masks but, even so, they're not staying in there long,' Winter said to her as though trying to excuse her discomfort.

She said nothing, instead concentrating on her surroundings. Saskia walked to the end of the corridor, a shaft of natural light came from the ceiling just before the next doorway, illuminating a square hole in the wall that had some cut wires leading into it. Possibly some kind of communications system for the bunker complex. That light helped in part to illuminate the second room which was smaller and empty apart from another swastika graffitied onto its wall.

'What was this place used for?' Saskia asked Winter.

'Ammunition bunker for the big gun up there on the cliff edge.'

That made sense, the slope led to and from the huge gun and whatever ammunition it used would have been heavy.

'Would it be possible to turn off your lights just for a minute so that I can get a better feel for what it would have been like at the time of the murder?'

'Of course,' Winter said. 'Lee, do you wanna turn those lights off for a minute and take a breather for five please?' he spoke into the first doorway.

'With pleasure,' a disembodied voice said, closely followed

by the doorway turning dark and then the white-suited Lee exiting out into the fresh air.

'Sunrise was about five-thirty. The Millers, who found the body, arrived here approximately eight a.m.. We've put a call out for dog walkers who might have been in the vicinity earlier. But time of death was one-thirty a.m. at the earliest, and, from the temperature of the deceased, we're estimating he'd been gone a good couple of hours before they found him. So, that's unlikely to be before sunrise, although possibly just as the sun rose. Either way, although there's daylight in this main corridor, very little gets into that particular room.'

'Perhaps that was why they chose that room. The victim is also turned away from them. Both suggest the killer didn't want to see him when they were shooting.'

'Which could suggest someone they knew quite well,' Winter joined in her thought process.

'Most likely. If it was just that they were squeamish then I doubt they'd have done it in such close proximity.'

'Agreed. We're trying to seize everyone who was at the party's clothing because there'd have been blood splatters on them.'

'It's execution style,' Saskia added. 'Do you know what weapon was used yet?'

'Not yet. We've certainly not found anything.'

'So why here? If you want to kill someone, why trek across fields or drive to a disused German war bunker?'

'Away from houses, underground so it might muffle the noise,' Winter suggested. 'We'll be testing that theory once Forensics have finished and we've been able to move Mr Cabot.'

'Or perhaps there's a more symbolic reason...' Saskia was still thinking aloud. 'I presume you're not suspecting organised crime, or a professional hit man? It seems a little too theatrical for that.'

'It's something we have to consider, but I agree, why here like this? It could certainly be significant.'

'Unless someone is suggesting he's a Nazi sympathiser, although from what you're saying that's not his style.'

'Again, that's something we will have to look into and that fits in more with what the DCI is thinking, but it doesn't sit right with me from what I know of the man.'

'Unless his killer is mentally ill and not rational like you,' Saskia suggested.

'Yes,' Winter sighed. 'At this stage we don't have a clue. It could be a total random stranger killing. Paul might have gone for a walk on his own and just bumped into someone here. Or maybe it's an individual who knows him and was angry at him being elected, or simply a personal dispute that just happened to come to a head last night.'

'As you said, an open mind. I'd like to see the house where the party was held if that's possible? And find out more about him and who was there with him.'

'Absolutely. We've got a team over there now and I'd like to take a proper look around too. Only visited briefly earlier. Then we can head back to the station because we're having a catch-up in two hours to take a look at what we have so far.' Winter had started to walk outside and back up the slope, but stopped and turned to look at her. 'That's if you're still OK, time-wise?'

'Yes of course,' Saskia replied, grateful to be back out in the sun after the concrete prison. She needed context now, to get to know the victim and his life a bit better, as well as the circumstances immediately prior to his murder. That way she could work backwards and try to understand who would want to execute Paul Cabot.

FIVE

THURSDAY

Winter drove his car to the Cabot farm house with Saskia following on her motorbike. He found that his eyes kept going to the rear-view mirror. If he was honest with himself, he'd have preferred it if she was next to him in the passenger seat. Seeing her again this afternoon had reminded him just how much he enjoyed being in her company.

The farmhouse wasn't just one dwelling, but a large main house with several granite outbuildings and, across the fields, another slightly smaller farmhouse.

'The brother lives in that one.' Winter had nodded to the smaller house in the distance, once they'd both disembarked and met in the courtyard. 'There's a granny annexe on this house – a dower cottage – but the father's passed and the mother is in a care home so it's not got anyone living in it at the moment, although it's still full of their belongings. Son and wife live here in the main house with Paul.'

He waited as Saskia stood and looked at the house. It was a classic Jersey farmhouse, rich chestnut orange and pink granite with white-painted wooden sash windows. A small sill-like porch was over the front door.

'He's got about two hundred and twenty-five vergees of land here too,' Winter added but then saw Saskia's puzzled look. 'Sorry, that's Jersey land measurements – it's about a hundred acres. This place has been with his family for generations. Real old Jersey.'

'Does he farm?'

'I believe the brother manages the farming side of things. Most of the fields get rented to one of the potato growers, or are used for growing livestock feed, or grazing cattle or horses.'

'What are these outbuildings used for now then?' Saskia asked. 'Why go all the way to Noirmont if you could go inside one of these outbuildings, which are solid granite and would muffle the noise of the gunshot? I'm still thinking Noirmont holds more significance.'

'The killer could have also used a quieter method of execution if noise was the only issue. A gunshot would have been loud in the silence of the night, but they've got double glazing on the windows and the killer could have muffled the sound with something if it was the only reason.'

'Greater risk of being seen by leaving here and going across to the bunker, so the more I think about it, the more significant that location is to the killer. The other factor is that it was execution style. That might be another indicator of motive,' Saskia replied.

Winter was enjoying the out-loud thinking and brainstorming that they'd naturally fallen into. He waited until she'd finished looking around the yard.

'We need to put protective clothing on again before we go inside,' he said to her getting two forensic oversuits and boots from the car. 'I don't want to cross-contaminate with the crime scene.'

'Of course,' Saskia replied.

He wondered if her mind had gone back to the concrete bunker and its terrible remains too. The smell seemed to have embedded itself in his nostrils, despite his oil. Perhaps he was becoming immune to its scent; might be time to upgrade.

Winter led Saskia into the house and straight to what had been Paul Cabot's study. 'Vicky, Paul's wife, their son, Daniel, and a family friend who was here when we arrived this morning, have all gone to Matthew Cabot's, the brother's house I pointed out from the yard,' Winter explained as they walked into the study. A forensic officer was inspecting a broken painting propped up on a chair. 'Morning, Andrew,' Winter said to him.

The man looked up at his voice and took a double-take at Saskia. Andrew had already annoyed her the first time they'd met with his sexist comments. Winter had spoken to him about it afterwards, pointing out the inappropriateness of his manner. He'd seemed to take it on board, but Winter felt himself hold his breath in case he tried it again. Winter had been a hair's breadth away from reporting him last time but now he knew Saskia a little better, he suspected that her wrath might be worse than any official sanction.

'Winter. Miss Monet,' Andrew replied.

There was no antagonism in his manner, in fact Winter could detect a note of respect towards Saskia that certainly hadn't been there before. Word of how she'd profiled the Pied Piper so accurately had obviously got around. He relaxed.

'Found anything interesting yet?' Winter asked him.

'As far as prints go, there was a party here last night with up to a dozen people, so it's going to take time to record all their prints and start eliminating and tracking them to see if anyone else has been in here. I've got prints on the frame here, three sets. I understand that Vicky Cabot came in here first thing looking for her husband, and then a family friend who stayed over was also in here. They moved it off the floor, so I'm hoping that the third set aren't from the victim.'

'OK thanks, Andrew, we OK to look around?'

'Sure, all recorded in here.' Andrew looked again at Saskia before returning his concentration to the picture and frame.

'So, Vicky Cabot woke up at around seven-thirty this morning,' Winter said, filling Saskia in on the morning's movements. 'She didn't think Paul had come to bed and so she came downstairs to look for him. Found this in the study, a family friend, Tom le Feuvre asleep on the sofa, and Paul's campaign manager, Joshua Redpath, asleep in the spare room. Neither men had seen Paul. They had both drunk a fair bit of alcohol and were sleeping it off. She said that wasn't unexpected as it had been a long night and a big celebration. She thought maybe her husband had got up early to either go and get some fresh croissants, which he used to get from the corner store, or do something relating to his new role as deputy. She didn't check to see if his car was still here and couldn't see that it was still parked in the garage. She'd then set about tidying up, starting in the kitchen, and about an hour later we arrived to tell her the news. Joshua had gone before we arrived, but Tom was still here.'

'Who is the painting of?' Saskia asked. She was peering at it, trying to see the face that had been ripped into several pieces.

'Paul's grandfather, Philippe Cabot. A real tough old Jersey farmer who stayed during the occupation and built up the family business afterwards.

'Fair bit of brute force used to wrench it off the wall and then slash it,' Andrew joined in the conversation. 'Looks likely that they used a letter opener which was on the desk. We've bagged it up already.'

'Does he resemble Paul? Could somebody have mistaken the portrait as one of him?' Saskia enquired.

Both men squinted at the torn painting of a distinguished-looking man.

'No. You can see a hint of a resemblance, but they definitely look quite different,' Winter replied.

'And the letter knife, was that sharp enough to stab a person with?'

Winter was impressed with Saskia's line of thinking.

'I'd say, yes. It was a posh one, not one of those cheap souvenir types. You can see how clean the cuts are on the canvas. That could easily have been someone's skin and soft flesh,' Andrew replied.

'Which means,' added Winter, 'that assuming this is connected to his killing, we go back again to why go to the bunker? If the killer could have stabbed Paul here, which would have been silent, why did he shoot him at the bunker?'

'A gun is less visceral and intimate than using a knife,' Saskia said. 'The style of killing already suggests that the killer knew Paul and didn't want to look at him when he shot him. Stabbing is much more personal, you have to plunge the knife into somebody and feel that impact. It's one thing being angry and slashing a painting, quite another to plunge a knife into someone you know, unless you're blind with rage or fear.'

'We don't know yet if the killer did this, it could have been Paul himself.'

'Mmmh, exactly,' Saskia replied. 'Anything else disturbed?'

'Not that we are aware of yet.'

'It's not as if this could have been randomly grabbed in rage, it was clearly targeted,' Saskia thought out loud again, looking around the room which otherwise looked untouched.

'Which means it's even more likely that the killer was here and they left together to go to the bunker.'

'Yet none of the other four occupants of the house heard anything!' Saskia said.

'There's a gun safe in the utility room,' Andrew said to Winter. 'Locked.'

'Right, I'll get on to Vicky, see if she has the code. Have you dusted it for fingerprints?'

Andrew raised his eyebrows.

'Of course you have, great.'

Winter called their family liaison officer, who he knew was with Vicky and her son, Daniel, at Matthew Cabot's house.

'Amanda, how are they doing?'

'So-so. In shock still, I'd say. I don't think it's sunk in.'

'Is Vicky in any fit state to tell me the combination to the gun safe?' Winter had walked through from the study to the utility and was now standing in front of a dark-grey steel cabinet.

'Hang on, I'll ask.' While Winter waited, he looked around the room he was in. The floor was granite – not an issue in the summer, but he'd bet it was cold in the winter. A lot of these really old farmhouses didn't have foundations, so damp could also be a problem. He saw no signs of any damp though in here. It was a neat and tidy middle-class utility area. An ironing board was folded up on the wall, Miele washing machine and tumble dryer, plus a tall fridge-freezer which obviously filled in as kitchen overflow. Winter had a quick look inside — half of the fridge contained alcohol and a few soft drinks, including three bottles of champagne.

The walls of the utility were rough granite, with dressed granite quoins, or corner stones, painted white around the window. Winter had already noticed the dripstones, the little sills that sat out from near the base of the chimneys outside, which meant the roof would have once been thatched. That indicated this was one of the older properties, perhaps as early as seventeenth century. He wondered what it must be like to know that generations of your family have lived in a home and to never move yourself.

'Winter, are you ready?' Amanda's voice came into his ear and he quickly stepped back to the lock on the safe.

'Yup, right in front of it,' he replied. It was one of the older-style gun safes, not a fancy biometric modern one, with just four numbers as the combination.

'OK, seven, nine, eight, two.'

'Seven, nine, eight, two,' Winter repeated as he worked the lock. When he entered the last digit, he felt the lock go loose and he was able to pull the door open. 'Got it, thanks Amanda.'

Inside were three shotguns, a modern handgun, and an old leather holster that was handgun shaped. The strap closing the holster was open and loose. Winter felt a buzz in his gut. He already had gloves on and so he carefully reached out and delicately slipped the gun from the holster. Being incredibly careful where he held it, even with gloves on, he sniffed the barrel. There was a slight odour. He couldn't be sure, but this gun smelt like it could have recently been fired. Was it the murder weapon?

'Andrew!' Winter shouted through to the forensics officer in the study. While he waited for him to respond, Winter checked the other hand gun. It was clean, smelling of the oil used to maintain guns with. Within seconds Andrew had arrived.

'What you found?'

'I think this pistol has been fired recently. It could be our murder weapon.'

Andrew came round to the front of the gun cabinet and looked at the holster and pistol inside.

'I slipped it out of the holster which was undone. No obvious signs of blood spatter but it might have been wiped.'

'Right, on it,' Andrew replied. 'Looks like one of those German guns from the Second World War.'

Saskia walked through the doorway, to see what they were discussing.

'German pistol from the occupation and I think it's been fired recently,' he said to her.

'Interesting,' she said, coming alongside him.

'Can you check for blood traces in all the sinks and bathroom,' Winter said to Andrew.

'Would they have washed it in water?' Saskia asked.

'No, more likely wiped it but whoever shot Paul Cabot would have received some blood spatters and gunshot residue on them. If they came back here to get rid of the gun then I'm betting they washed their hands at the same time,' Winter said to Saskia. 'And, Andrew, can you make sure everyone who was at that party is contacted and their clothing from yesterday seized. I'm going to go and have another chat with Vicky, Paul's brother, and his friend Tom Le Feuvre. Tom hasn't been home so I'll get his clothes bagged and find out from the others where theirs are. If this is the murder weapon, then chances are that whoever the killer is, they were comfortable with moving around this house, which means it's most likely a friend or family member.'

SIX

THURSDAY

Saskia had looked around the Cabot house while Winter dealt with the gun in the safe. It was one of those homes in which the family were steeped like tea stains into its very fabric. She expected that somewhere, perhaps inside a cupboard or on a door frame, she'd find some lines marked with names alongside, a height record of the many children that had grown up in the house. There were window frames scored and tables gouged, each scar carrying with it a story or memory of its making and its maker. She suspected that the sofas and chairs in the living room, gathered around the huge granite fireplace like guests at a tea party, were more than one generation old. Their upholstery was new, the stuffing replaced, but the styles were traditional and the frames showed the decades of use they'd been subjected to. This family clearly enjoyed and protected its heritage.

Paintings of the island were on the walls, photographs of what were probably family members in traditional island dress next to Jersey cows or one of the tall Jersey cabbages. The plants which were once grown all over the island, reached six to ten feet in height, their stems often made into walking sticks. This home was like a potted history of the island, told lovingly through one family.

A photograph of what she presumed to be Daniel, Paul's son and the family's future, was on the sideboard with his father standing next to him, arm proudly around his shoulders. She hadn't got to see the victim's face, but it was him. She knew that from the campaign posters which were stacked in one corner of the living room, presumably from where they'd been dumped there last night after the election. A smiling Paul Cabot had looked out at her, sandwiched in-between the words, *Vote Paul Cabot for Deputy*. She couldn't tell what kind of a man he had been from that photograph – it was a marketing shot designed to pull in votes. The house gave her far more clues.

'I'm heading over now to talk to Vicky, Paul's wife, do you want to come?' Winter stuck his head round the door.

'Yes, that might be useful,' she'd replied, and followed him from the house. There was going to be a lot to look into with this murder, and while there was always the chance that the political aspect was a motive, something told her it ran far deeper than that.

Vicky Cabot looked exactly as Saskia would expect a woman in shock to look. She was sitting on the sofa in Matthew and Gill Cabot's house, with a cup of cold tea on the small table by her side. The house was hushed, life with the volume control turned right down, and everyone meandered around slowly and aimlessly, like leaves floating on a windless pond, severed from their reality. In the room with Vicky was another woman, her sister-in-law, Gill, and a man, Tom, hair wrung through with grey, but with the body and complexion of someone who led an active life.

'Matthew and Daniel are walking the dogs,' Gill said to

Winter and Saskia by way of explanation – DC Amanda Potter had already informed them when she'd answered the door.

'I'm DI Winter Labey,' he said addressing Gill. 'I spoke to Mrs Cabot and Mr Le Feuvre earlier, but I have a few more questions for you all. Were you at the party last night Mrs Cabot?'

Gill let out a big shivering sigh. 'Yes, of course. We were at the parish hall early on in the evening and then all went back to Vicky and Paul's to wait for the results.'

'What time did you leave?'

'Not long after the results came through. We don't have the stamina like we used to I'm afraid. Both of us were tired.'

'So that was what, eleven-thirty?'

'No. More like twelve-thirty.'

'Who was still there when you left?'

'Oh gosh, let me think. Besides Vicky and Matthew obviously, Tom,' she nodded to the man sitting on the other chair, 'and Joshua Redpath. His wife had left earlier. Apparently needed to go and relieve the babysitter. Then there was the businessman, Frank Mason, and the young lad who helped Paul with his social media, Alfie. I think that was it.'

'George was there too,' Vicky spoke up, her voice cracked and strained. 'He's an old school friend of Paul's. Didn't leave until after I'd gone to bed.'

'Thank you,' Winter said to them both. 'We are trying to eliminate DNA, fingerprints, and other trace evidence, and so if you don't mind we would like to take all of your fingerprints and DNA. Would any of you have any objections?'

He looked around the room. Saskia watched everyone's faces as they all shook their heads, shrugged their shoulders, or said 'fine'.

'When will you need this?' Tom spoke up. 'I'm going to have to head off in about an hour, unless you need me any longer, Vicky?' he said to her.

'No, it's fine. You've been so good, thank you.'

'I can get someone here in the next half hour to get your samples but, Mr Le Feuvre, before you go, we would like to ask everyone who stayed overnight at the property, or was one of the last guests to leave, if they would allow us to examine the clothing they wore. I understand you've not been home to get changed yet, so would you agree to us doing that?'

'You're not suggesting Tom had anything to do with this!' Vicky's voice was raised. 'He and Paul were at prep school together, they've been life-long friends.'

'I'm not suggesting anyone is a suspect, Mrs Cabot, but by eliminating people from our enquiry, it enables us to get a clearer picture of what went on and where people were.'

'Vicky, it's fine. I'm more than happy for you to have my clothes, Detective Inspector. If it helps,' Tom reassured her.

'I can lend you something of Matthew's until you get home,' Gill said to him, smiling gently.

'I will need your shoes too. All of you,' Winter added.

'No problem,' Tom replied.

Saskia could see no concern in anyone's demeanour at the requests. They clearly didn't expect Winter to find anything untoward.

'I'll get you some clothes now,' Gill said, standing. It was obvious she was eager to get away from the stifling atmosphere in the room.

'Before you do, I'd also like to ask you all if any of you saw the broken picture in Mr Cabot's study last night?'

Gill shook her head.

'Vicky and I came across it this morning,' Tom said. 'But that was the first I'd seen it like that. I think at some point I'd probably gone in there during the evening yesterday and it had been fine.'

'And have any of you thought of anybody or any reason as to

why this might have happened? I know we spoke earlier, but has something come to mind since?'

All three of them shook their heads.

'And, finally, do you know if there was ever any controversy surrounding Philippe Cabot, especially during the war?'

'Absolutely not,' a voice came from behind Winter, and a man that Saskia presumed to be Matthew Cabot walked in through the door.

'Our grandfather was not only a hard worker, but he was a good man. He hid a radio from the Nazis and used to deliver vegetables to neighbours along with the news from off island. There was never any impropriety on his part I can assure you of that! Our family stuck the war out here and didn't leave, unlike some. They kept the farm going despite the hardships and helped look after their fellow islanders.'

'Thank you, Mr Cabot, I wasn't suggesting he was a sympathiser or collaborator, but I do have to ask these questions because I don't understand why the painting of him has been damaged.

'Well that's obvious. Jealousy. Our grandfather built up the family fortunes and we have been the benefactors of that. There's plenty of jealous types who thought Paul entitled. You only need to look at some of the comments on social media during the election. *He's alright, he has a big house and loads of land, what does he know about the struggle to buy a property or make ends meet.* That kind of thing.'

'We will of course be looking into all the social media messages like that from during the campaign.'

'You should speak to Alfie then, he knows every one of them,' Matthew added. 'Had to deal with their vitriol for weeks.'

'It was only a very small minority,' Vicky said, looking at her brother-in-law. 'Most of the comments were very supportive, that's why Paul got voted in, topped the poll in St Brelade. People liked him, they knew he loved this parish and the island.'

'Of course, Vick, I'm not suggesting...' Matthew tailed off, deflating as though she'd pulled the plug from out of his air valve.

'It's always just a small vocal minority, and they usually don't just target one individual either. Some of them we're aware of,' Winter interjected, trying to ease the tension. 'But if there's anybody who you believe was particularly focused on Paul then please let us have their names.'

Behind Matthew in the doorway, the pale face of Daniel Cabot appeared. He looked drawn and tired, dark circles under his eyes, his head hanging. Matthew stepped out of the way to let him enter, but his nephew slipped away again. Saskia wondered if it was a standard teenage aversion to adults, or that he was unable to cope with the heavy conversation.

'Vicky I need to ask you who had access to the gun safe,' Winter asked directly.

Saskia realised this was the primary reason for their visit. Winter could have asked the family liaison to collect the clothes and samples.

'Guns...' she trailed off and Saskia wasn't sure if she'd forgotten the question or was just struggling to answer. 'Paul and Daniel used it mostly,' Vicky eventually continued.

'But you knew the combination?' Winter pressed.

'No... well yes, it's written down somewhere at home but Daniel was the one who gave it to me earlier. Tom, you and George sometimes go shooting with Paul, don't you, but I'm not sure if you ever had the code to the safe?'

'No, never had any need to,' Tom confirmed.

'Where is the code written, Mrs Cabot? Could somebody have found it?'

'Highly unlikely, detective, it's upstairs in our bedroom but it's actually our wedding date. I'd forgotten that until Daniel told me earlier.'

'So somebody might have known that?'

'No, why would they? I think Paul chose it because it was an easy number for him to remember.'

'Was there any reason why the gun safe would have been unlocked last night?'

'Absolutely not. Everyone had been drinking, we wouldn't consider handling dangerous firearms under those circumstances,' Vicky replied.

'OK, I know everyone has been asked to give individual statements and at this very difficult time please let us know if you encounter any issues. The media are bound to get in contact. I wouldn't be surprised if the UK national press are interested as well as our local journalists. Detective Constable Potter is your point of contact but you also have my number too.'

'When can we see him?' The voice came from the doorway. Daniel must have been hanging around outside listening. Saskia saw the flicker of sympathy go across Winter's face.

'I'm sorry but I can't answer that right now. We need to ensure that our investigation is very thorough and so your father will be seen by the pathologist so that we can discover as much about the circumstances of his death as possible.'

Saskia wondered if the family would ever be able to view the remains. She'd not looked too closely at the head wound, but from the mess on the wall and floor, she suspected there might be too much damage. She also suspected that Winter knew that but it would be a bridge he'd have to cross at another time.

SEVEN

THURSDAY

'What do you think about the family?' Winter asked Saskia once they'd arrived at the police station and were climbing the stairs to the office.

'There's an undercurrent of friction there – not unusual in most family dynamics, but Matthew was very defensive of the grandfather and I detected a slight tension between him and Vicky... but that could just be emotions running high.'

'Yeah, I agree. We also need to keep in mind that it might not have been the killer who smashed the painting. It could have been Paul, and that was the catalyst for an argument and his death.'

'You think his brother could have killed him?'

'I think everyone is a suspect right now until I can categorically gather evidence to say they're not.

'Why do you think Paul had so many guns?' Saskia asked.

'Sounds like he did some rabbit shooting and possibly pheasant. They're protected here, but they're not native and can be quite destructive with the crops, so farmers get permission to keep numbers down. Also, owning guns isn't unusual here. Compared to the United Kingdom, Jersey has a lot more guns per head of population. There's about thirteen-hundred firearms certificate holders – that means over ten percent of the population. Some say it's because of our history. The Jersey Militia had defended the island for generations from the constant French attempts to invade, and then the German occupation showed just how possible it was for the island to lose its freedom. That leaves a collective sense of needing to have some kind of protection to hand.'

'I never realised the island had so many guns,' Saskia replied.

'Oh don't get me wrong, we're not in the league of the US – I think they've got more guns than people. We're just over nine guns per one hundred people, it's just that's more than double the United Kingdom. We're not exactly murder island here – gun crime is incredibly rare and our crime rates are mercifully low. Thankfully, or I'd never get a holiday.'

They'd reached Winter's desk by this time and Saskia sat down on the chair he'd pulled up for her. On his desk was a white paper bag with something inside that was leaching grease. A pink Post-it note was attached:

To keep you going. L

Winter picked it up and peered inside.

'Mmmhhmm,' he said, beaming a big smile. 'Jam doughnut. Would you like some?' he asked Saskia.

'No thanks,' she reassured him and didn't miss the delight at her reply on his face. She'd never been a fan of doughnuts, so it wasn't martyrdom.

'I'm just going to go and wash my hands first,' he said to her, 'need to get the crime scene off my skin.'

That she could totally understand.

'Cheers, Lisa,' Winter shouted across the bank of desks to a young detective who gave him the thumbs up in return.

Saskia suddenly felt a tiny twinge of something in her gut. Was that jealousy? She'd found herself assessing the female detective in terms of attractiveness and decided that she was reasonably likely to be a woman that would appeal to men. Surely she wasn't getting territorial over DI Labey? Saskia admonished herself. It wasn't as if she could even entertain a romantic liaison with him anyway. Her brother was one huge barrier to that happening. There could only ever be one man in her life.

'Miss Monet, back again?' Winter's boss, Detective Chief Inspector Chris Sharpe, had crept up on her.

She smiled pleasantly at him, knowing she didn't need to reply to that. He'd been dead against her helping out on the Pied Piper inquiry, and he was no doubt here to undermine her and Winter again.

'You've been to the crime scene?' he asked, but didn't wait for an answer – he obviously knew she had. 'What do you think? You and I both have experience of the UK political scene. Politics over here is an amateur mess compared to Parliament, but please don't quote me on that.'

He smiled at her conspiratorially, showing a partially blackened incisor tooth. She'd not noticed that before and tried not to stare at it. He was a tall man and loomed over her, which afforded a good view up his large nostrils that she could have done without. He was behaving differently today – perhaps he'd only recently found out that she was newly over from England, like him, and thought the two of them could form an alliance against what he thought to be the somewhat luddite locals?

He pulled up Winter's chair and sat down, leaning his elbows on his knees and looking at her expectantly. 'I'm thinking it could be a Jo Cox or David Amess-style attack.'

Saskia knew he was referring to the female member of parliament who'd been shot by a far right activist, and the male one targeted because of his voting record, by another terrorist.

'I'm not so sure yet,' Saskia said. She could have fudged her reply, made sure she didn't engage his wrath immediately, but she was never one for avoiding a situation. Far better to get things straight out in the open. 'I need to get to know the victim better first,' she qualified, 'but I think it's more personal, more deep-rooted. I think he knew his killer.'

'Well, it's quite likely he *did* know his killer. It's a small island you know,' the DCI said, slapping his knees with his hands and sitting up straight. I think we're going to find that one of his proposed policies has rubbed somebody up the wrong way. You can't tell me that the fact he's murdered on the night he's elected, isn't connected.'

Saskia got the impression that the DCI far preferred the closed question one-way style of conversation, rather than an actual debate. Winter walked up to them at this point and thankfully broke the deadlock.

'Sir,' Winter said to him.

'Ah, DI Labey, ready for the briefing now?'

'Yes, of course.'

'Good, just been chatting with Miss Monet here about the obvious political motive for Paul Cabot's murder. Miss Monet seems to think it's someone he knew, so that list of activists who have been targeting the hustings and the online trolls should be our first priority.'

Saskia saw Winter's eyes flick briefly towards her before returning to a steady stare at the DCI.

'Let's get to it then, round everyone up, would you?' the DCI said, ignoring the tension.

There was a steady hum of information exchange all around Saskia as she sat waiting for the rest of the team to file into the briefing room. Winter and DCI Sharpe were up front.

'Hi, good to see you back,' Detective Sergeant Jonathon Vibert said to Saskia, sitting in the seat next to her.

'Thanks.' She smiled warmly. Jonno was a man without any front to him, what you saw was what you got and she knew he was good friends with Winter. She felt comfortable around him.

'Right, everyone, let's get started,' DCI Sharpe barked from the front. The room instantly fell silent. This was a murder inquiry and the first twenty-four hours of any case like this were essential. They needed to move as fast as they could to get the best results and everyone knew that.

'As most of you know, Detective Superintendent Graeme Walker has been signed off sick for the next couple of weeks and so I'm acting up. I will have oversight of this case, but DI Labey will be the investigating officer. The fact that our victim was just voted in as a deputy of St Brelade last night is going to ensure plenty of media interest and I don't need to tell you all that anyone caught talking to the press will be on Traffic duties when I catch them.'

No one reacted to the DCI's warning – the team were well aware that Jersey's closed-knit community ensured that you couldn't mention anything without that person knowing someone involved, or somebody who knew somebody who was involved. Discretion was a prerequisite.

Winter stood up and addressed the room. 'So, our victim, Paul Cabot, as the DCI has said, was elected as deputy of St Brelade last night, after which he and a select group of friends went back to his house to celebrate. We know that Mr Cabot was still alive and well when his wife went to bed at just gone one a.m. His body was found by Mr and Mrs Miller at the Noirmont bunkers at approximately eight a.m. The call to emergency services was 8.07. What we don't know is what happened in the seven hours that led to Mr Cabot's death.

'He was shot in the head at close range by a pistol firing 9mm bullets. There is a World War Two German Walther P38 pistol and 9 by 19mm Parabellum rounds in the gun safe at Mr Cabot's house. I suspect that this pistol has recently been fired and it's now with Forensics. If that is the gun used to shoot Paul Cabot, the killer must have taken it from the house and then returned after he'd killed him. We have seized the clothing of anybody that we know was at the house overnight, including his campaign manager and a friend.'

'What about the wife? Isn't she a suspect?' a detective spoke up from the back. 'How do we know she didn't get up and kill him?'

'You're right, Pete, we don't and that's why Vicky and their son Dominic's clothes have also been taken in by Forensics and the premises searched in case of attempted disposal. Whoever shot Paul would have had firearms discharge and blood on them. Forensics have told me trace elements of blood were found in the downstairs toilet sink. Stands to reason that the killer would have cleaned up the gun and themselves when they got back. The only sign of anything untoward having taken place is the painting of Philippe Cabot, Paul's grandfather, in his study. It's been ripped from the wall and slashed in anger. Now we don't know if that was Paul or his attacker, or even something unrelated. Everyone present at the party denies the attack and nobody saw the damaged painting until the morning. Who was looking into the grandfather's history?'

'Me, sir,' DC Peter Edwards spoke from behind again. 'Absolutely nothing to suggest he was anything but highly respected. The family all stayed behind to see out the occupation. There are testimonials from neighbours and island officials saying that they helped to feed some of those who couldn't help themselves, and, after the war, Philippe became head of the parish. Respectable and loved his island by all accounts. Not a whiff of scandal.'

'Then why attack the painting?' Winter asked the room, not expecting an answer.

'You're focusing on the party guests, but it could be a third party,' DCI Sharpe said now.

Winter turned his attention to the DCI.

'That's correct, sir, and we are keeping an open mind, but if the Walther P38 is the murder weapon then the fact that the killer persuaded Mr Cabot to walk to the bunker, and also moved around his house seemingly openly, suggests it was someone familiar to him. If you've just shot a man, you don't then go back to the house, replace the gun and clean yourself up, risking being spotted by one of the family or a friend without a reason and excuse to be there. You chuck the gun over the cliff and get out of there.'

'I don't believe in coincidences, DI Labey, and that means we have to take very seriously the fact it was the night Paul Cabot was elected. We know that there were several individuals who were targeting him online and at hustings, although he wasn't the only politician in their sights.'

'Indeed, sir, and we are looking into every one of them.'

Saskia was impressed with DI Labey's patience. The DCI so obviously had it in for him, but he wasn't wavering in his conviction.

'And what about the swastikas on the wall in the bunker?' The DCI challenged Winter. 'Is that not someone suggesting either he was too right wing, or that the killer was?'

'We've had confirmation from the Channel Island Occupation Society, who look after the bunkers, that they knew about the graffiti. It appeared about two weeks ago, but as they're volunteers, they just hadn't got round to cleaning it up. It's not the first time. Kids go up there drinking sometimes. We've received reports of broken bottles and anti-social behaviour before now.'

'Well I think we can't ignore the very obvious political aspect of this crime and who's to say the killer hadn't put the graffiti on the walls before that night. They could have been stalking Paul Cabot. They might have attacked the grandfather's painting because he was also a politician, wasn't he?'

'A Connétable, yes, and you're right of course, sir,' Winter replied with practised calm. 'We have a lot more people to interview. I'm happy that we've gathered the forensic materials that we need. Now we need to talk to everyone in more detail and hope that the lab comes back with some results for us quickly.'

Saskia knew that politics could be polarising, fanatics were everywhere and so it wasn't beyond the realms of possibility that there was one in Jersey who had killed Paul, but something in her gut told her that wasn't their killer. Trouble was, gut feelings were totally useless in a murder inquiry, she needed facts and evidence if she was to help DI Labey to solve the case.

EIGHT

THURSDAY

There was one man who had played a key role in Paul Cabot's election bid, and that was his campaign manager, Joshua Redpath. The team had been trying to contact Joshua by telephone, but had no luck. It alerted Winter's detective senses and after the team briefing, he'd gone straight to the antiques shop Joshua owned, eager to find out if they had a killer, or another victim, on their hands. The combination of the political connection, and the opportunity he had from being in the house overnight, meant Joshua was a clear potential suspect.

As it turned out, Joshua Redpath was there – looking very much alive and well, although a little drawn and tired.

Winter walked into Joshua Redpath's antique shop, and, without looking at a single price tag, knew it was the kind of place he'd not be able to afford a thing. He was definitely not the target customer. From rich mahogany grandfather clocks to ostentatious vases and paintings that needed more wall space than his little flat could afford, it was a shop for Jersey's wealthier residents. He stopped and admired a large bronze statue of two horses galloping. It would take up half his sitting room.

Joshua was talking to a customer when Winter arrived and so he'd waited, browsing some of the art on the walls. There was an Edmund Blampied print, an artist from Jersey who was fondly collected in the island. Winter thought this particular one a little too dark for his tastes and he much preferred the more cheerful watercolour of a little girl and her dog walking across a beach with Gorey Castle in the distance. The unknown artist had captured the expression on her face perfectly, a combination of innocence and mischief in one.

'Can I help you?' A woman approached Winter with a smile.

'I need to speak with Mr Redpath.' Winter returned the smile but didn't offer up his name. Announcing that he was a police detective and asking to speak to Mr Redpath in front of customers and staff would be guaranteed to get the Jersey tongues wagging.

Winter watched her walk across to Joshua and let him know that Winter was waiting. There next ensued around ten minutes of what Winter could only describe as masterful tactics on how to totally ignore the fact the person you are talking to is trying to escape. He could see Joshua clearly explaining to the elderly man that he needed to go and speak to Winter, but the man wasn't going to let him go. He kept him talking and each time Joshua tried to step away, he launched into another conversation. Joshua was too polite, or perhaps just not assertive enough, to cut the elderly man off. Winter was about to intervene when Joshua finally managed to extricate himself from the customer.

'So sorry, what can I do for you?' Joshua said coming across to him, hand extended.

'I wonder if we could have a word in private, Mr Redpath,' Winter said to him. 'Detective Inspector Winter Labey.' He wasn't sure how much the man knew; whether Vicky or one of the others had called him. They hadn't released the victim's name to the media yet, but that didn't mean anything in this island. Rumours could spread faster than the tides coming in, leaving you cut off and unable to manage how communications were managed.

'Of course, is something the matter? Has something happened?'

He seemed oblivious.

'Your family is fine,' Winter reassured him. It was often the first reaction of people when he told them he wanted to speak to them and what his name was: they immediately thought he might be the bearer of bad news. To be fair, there'd been quite a few times when he had been. 'We've been trying to contact you by phone,' Winter added.

'Ah yes, I left my phone in the office, haven't had a chance to check the answerphone either. Why don't you come through?'

Joshua turned and led him through the labyrinth of antiques, Winter being especially careful he didn't accidentally knock something off that might cost him a month's wages.

Winter thought it strange that on the day following an election in which Joshua had played an active role, that he hadn't been keeping up with island news. If he had, he'd know a body had been found at Noirmont. Or perhaps he already knew that because he'd put it there.

'Are you Willy Labey's son?' Joshua asked, breaking into his thoughts as he led him through to the back of the shop.

'Yes,' Winter replied, unsure of the connection between Redpath and his father, who was about twenty years older than the man.

'We were in the Round Table together for a while. Do send him my best wishes, won't you?' He waved Winter into a tiny office at the back and in particular to a seat which looked like it had once been one of a dinner table set.

'I will.'

'Would you like a drink? I'm parched. Mr Le Brun there doesn't go out much these days and so when he does you tend to get clobbered with all his stories. Don't get me wrong, they're interesting but I have heard them all before.'

As he talked, Joshua had filled up a small kettle in an equally tiny sink. 'Tea, coffee?' he asked again.

'Coffee would be great thank you,' Winter replied, noting that while Mr Le Brun might be in a talkative mood, so too was Joshua Redpath, who clearly didn't seem to enjoy periods of silence. Winter wondered if it might be nerves while he waited to hear why a police detective wanted to talk to him, or just how he always was.

Joshua carried on talking about the merits of instant freeze-dried coffee over cheap instant, until he'd set two mugs down on the desk in front of them and folded his tall, angular frame into a chair. He had the look of someone much older, as though life had somehow dried him out. It wasn't that his face was lined, or his hair completely grey or balding; it was an air of weariness about him. Finally, he succumbed to the inevitable revelations that Winter had come to share.

'I'm sorry to have to inform you, Mr Redpath, that Paul Cabot was found murdered this morning.'

The look on Joshua's face instantly told Winter that he clearly hadn't known.

'No. No, that's impossible. I was with him all last night. I stayed over at his house.' Joshua Redpath seemed to have shrivelled and paled in seconds.

'Did you see him this morning?' Winter asked.

'No... I didn't. I went to bed and left them to it, he'd just won the election you know. We were celebrating. This morning I had to open up here so I got up, went home for a shower and came straight here. I didn't see anyone, apart from Tom who was asleep on the sofa and to say goodbye to Vicky who had just woken up. Nobody else was downstairs. My God. Are you sure it's Paul? What happened?'

The cup of Instant freeze-dried coffee was forgotten. Joshua slumped in his chair and looked like a shocked and frightened school boy.

'What time did you leave, Mr Redpath?' Winter avoided his last questions.

'My alarm was set for...' Joshua seemed to search the room with his eyes as though his alarm time might be written on the wall. 'Where's my phone?' He opened his desk drawer and pulled out a mobile phone. 'Oh Lord, I have dozens of missed calls.' He seemed to freeze for a moment, his breathing speeding up as the shock washed through him.

'Are you alright, Mr Redpath?' Winter asked.

A moment later the man came to. 'Yes, yes, I'm fine. It's just a shock, you know? I was his campaign manager. Been spending virtually every day and evening with the man for weeks. Neglected this place to help him get elected. Alarm, wasn't it... seven-thirty a.m. the alarm was. I got straight up and drove home.'

'I'd have thought you might have taken the day off to celebrate,' Winter prompted.

'No. I needed to get back to work. I put so much time into that campaign, and now...'

Winter wondered if Joshua was less concerned about Paul's death than the fact his efforts to get someone elected had now gone to waste.

'What kind of a man was Paul Cabot?'

Joshua looked at him as though he'd asked him if the moon was square. 'Err, he was a good man.'

There were no tears or signs of upset. No gushing words of praise for his murdered friend. Perhaps Joshua was in shock? Winter would need to arrange another time to talk to him in more detail. For now, he'd concentrate on the most critical questions and gathering evidence.

'Did you go into Mr Cabot's study on your way out?'

'Study?' A wave of nerves washed over Redpath's face. 'No. No, like I said I just left.'

'So you weren't aware that a painting had been damaged in Paul's study?'

'No, no, I wasn't. No.'

Winter wasn't sure why Joshua Redpath might have lied about that, but he was sure he was lying. His body language and the fact he over-asserted his answer, leaked the fact he was unsure of his reply. Could he be their killer or was he simply panicking that he might become a suspect?

'Mr Redpath, we are asking everyone who was there at the house overnight to surrender the clothes they were wearing and give DNA and fingerprint samples. Would you agree to do that, please? It's just so that we can discount you all from the inquiry and get a clearer idea of everyone's movements and whether somebody else was in the house last night.'

'You mean the murderer was in the house?'

Winter said nothing and instead waited for the reply to his question.

'No, that's fine... I mean, yes absolutely I'd be happy to give samples and you can have my clothes.'

'Thank you. If you don't mind, I have an officer outside who will escort you home now to pick up the clothes and they can also take your DNA and fingerprints at the same time.'

'You want to go to my home? Now?'

'Just to get the clothes, Mr Redpath. We have mobile DNA and fingerprint kits. We can take those anywhere.'

Winter's eyes dropped to the still-open drawer of Joshua's desk, from where he'd taken his mobile phone. A photograph of a woman in an antique silver frame was lying on top. He wondered who she was and why she'd been relegated to the desk drawer instead of being in full view on top of it.

'I understand your wife was at the party too, Mr Redpath?'

'She was, yes. But she left earlier because we could only get a babysitter until eleven-thirty. It was a school night. Do you want her clothes too?'

'Just those who were at the house overnight, thank you. But I would like to talk to her at some point.'

'I'd better call her. She'll be at work.'

'Our investigations are ongoing at this stage, Mr Redpath, I'd like to talk to you again at some point.'

'Yes, fine... I'll be out in a few minutes,' Joshua said to Winter, eager to get on the phone, and a clear request that he have the conversation with his wife in private.

Winter left him to it and stepped outside, closing the door. He didn't however, immediately go back into the shop. Instead, he hung around outside the office door where he could just hear the stressed hushed tones of Joshua Redpath as he spoke to his wife.

'Annette, shut up, you know damned well why I wasn't answering my phone. Listen to me. Paul's dead... Yes. No, I'm not trying to wind you up. I'm serious. A police officer has just come to the shop and said he's been murdered... Don't be bloody ridiculous – and if you ever say that again... I'd suggest you keep your mouth shut about that, because it's not going to look good on any of us. Is it? I don't care, you brought that on yourself. They're going to want to talk to you too. Look, I've got to go because they're outside. We'll talk about it later and I will be home as usual.'

Winter heard the big sigh as Joshua ended his phone call, and so stepped away from the door and out the shop to brief the police officer waiting to take Joshua home. He wanted to make sure the officer used the photograph from last night's celebrations to double-check that the clothes Joshua was handing over were indeed the ones he'd worn last night. Winter hadn't been convinced about his answer regarding the painting in the study, and now that phone call made him a whole lot more suspicious. Joshua Redpath was clearly trying to hide something, but was it murder or another dark secret?

NINE

THURSDAY

After the briefing, Saskia stayed at the police station collating the information she needed, until Winter said he needed to go out. She took the opportunity to head home where she could read everything in peace. It was another perfect afternoon as she rode along the Five Mile Road that led across St Ouen's Bay. The tide was well on its way out so she couldn't be tempted to go surfing, but nature was more than enough of a relaxing scene after her busy day. The issue was that her brother was due for his weekly session tonight and that was usually anything but relaxing.

Her next-door neighbour, June, had her door open to allow the cool sea air to circulate around her cottage. It meant that Pushki, her Yorkshire Terrier, was able to come running out the house to greet Saskia. He bounced up at the small granite wall that separated their cottages, asking for some attention. Saskia was happy to oblige, stroking his soft ears and head and then his belly when he flung himself onto his back for the next level up of attention. Saskia could hear the television was on in June's sitting room and imagined she'd be sitting in her chair watching it.

When Saskia looked up, the indignant face of her cat, Bilbo, met her in her own sitting room window. She'd dared to give Pushki, a mere dog, first dibs at her attention and not him. She was in trouble. The only remedy would be some instant gratification with a treat, followed by dinner. Luckily Bilbo was easily won over by his stomach.

Once he was happy, Saskia turned her attentions to her own dinner, taking a vegetable lasagne out of the freezer and putting it in the microwave. She did cook from scratch, but she had to be in the mood.

Since coming to Jersey, she'd discovered the delights of the various seafood vans and sellers. A pot of fresh crab meat or some scallops to fry, was an easy meal. Her nearest seller, Faulkner Fisheries, also had a summer barbecue and she smelt the garlic prawns and grilled fish of the day wafting over when the wind was in the right direction. She was eager to try it out for herself one day, but for now she'd have to make do with her anaemic-looking vegetarian lasagne. She'd quite fancied a glass of Pinot Grigio with it, but that would have to wait until David had been.

His visits were essential to ensure he was keeping on the straight and narrow. She had to keep her wits about her and monitor his every expression and word, to look for any hidden clues that he was straying. As a high-functioning psychopath, David was currently doing well for himself. A good job with a hedge fund and a wealthy girlfriend. He hid within society and hadn't harmed it. Yet Saskia knew his need for excitement and his complete lack of fear of consequences meant she had to keep on reminding him that to continue living his nice lifestyle, he had to play by society's rules.

Pushki let her know David had arrived. The dog was a good judge of character and she opened the door to see David sneering at the barking Yorkshire Terrier as he walked up the path.

'One day,' he pointed his finger at the dog.

Just as Saskia was about to close the door, she caught a glimpse of a figure retreating up the lane. For a moment she thought it was Mark Byrne, the psychopathic prison officer from work. Then she chided herself for being so paranoid. What reason would he have for being here? She needed to get a grip and not allow him to get to her.

Saskia shut the door on her anxiety.

David had walked into her cottage without even a hello and flopped himself down onto her sofa as though he owned the place.

'Good evening, David,' she said to him purposefully.

'Good evening, Saskia,' he mirrored.

'Do you want a drink?' she asked him.

'No. Can't stay too long. Just clocking in for my weekly psycho assessment.'

He was being even more flippant than usual and that was rarely a good sign. He looked well; there seemed to be an extra glow about him. His hair was immaculate as usual, and his blue eyes weren't exactly sparkling, but they had more life to them than their usual iceberg stillness.

'So how have you been? Did Jackie have a good trip away?' Saskia asked.

'She's fine, but Allan's gone missing.'

'Allan?'

'Yeah, you know the driver who hangs about the place all the time? That's why I can't stay long. I think Jackie's going to call the police and report him missing. We've not seen him since Friday.'

'So he wasn't there when Jackie was away?' Saskia fished.

'Nope. I haven't buried him in the rose bushes, if that's what you're asking.' David smirked at her. 'I do listen to what you say,

Sas. Actions have consequences and all that, and I have to not be seen as anti-social or I could lose everything.'

She studied his face and body language as he said that. Was he really taking everything she said on board? Was he maturing and mellowing as she'd hoped? Her concern was that he said, *not be seen as anti-social*, rather than just not being anti-social. Had he done something that he'd covered up?

'So what do you think might have happened to Allan?' she asked David.

He shrugged. 'Bloke spent a few years in prison for armed robbery. Maybe his past caught up with him, or perhaps his boyfriend did him in. I heard them arguing.'

'Does it worry you that Jackie's calling in the police? I mean they might find it odd that it happened while she was away.'

'No. Why should it worry me? You know my record is clean, apart from those few minor things when I was a kid. Nothing else was ever public.'

Saskia knew that well enough. It hadn't been easy to keep his name clean and him out of trouble over the years. She knew she'd done things and said things that she shouldn't in order to protect her brother. It's what she did.

'If Jackie wants them to investigate then that's up to her.'

'Yeah but you know that you need to at least appear to be a bit concerned about it,' Saskia said to him, eyes narrowing. 'Otherwise they might suspect you.'

'I know.' He smiled at her. 'How's this?' David's face changed from its usual benign charm to a look of worrying anxiety 'I've been so concerned about him. He's always so reliable.' Then he stopped and his face relaxed back to a conceited smirk.

'Just don't overdo it,' Saskia said to him, 'And I hope Allan is OK.'

David shrugged.

Saskia had got used to the frustration she felt when dealing with her brother over the years. For a long time she'd just wanted to shake him and try to make him 'feel' something, but her career had helped her to come to terms with the fact he wasn't totally unique – there were others like him out there – and that she would never squeeze a drop of empathy from him.

David didn't stay long – he never did – and Saskia saw him out to ensure that Pushki wasn't terrorised. She watched her brother stride off down the path, not a care in the world.

* * *

David generally didn't mind the sessions with his sister, there was an order to them which he found reassuring. He also liked being the centre of attention, and found it quite useful to have a weekly reminder of what the lines were that he shouldn't cross in order to maintain his lifestyle. Of course, he was a lot smarter than she realised and he understood that it wasn't just what you did, but it was getting away with it that was key. Left to his own devices, he wouldn't have cared. That's why he wasn't bothered about the police investigating Allan's disappearance, he'd got it sussed. He'd been smart, thanks to Saskia's advice.

The memory of plunging the sharp knife into the back of Allan's neck sent a shiver of pleasure through his body. He'd reached his car and for a few seconds he leant on the roof, holding on to the tingle that had run through him. He really had done it perfectly. Allan's spinal cord had been severed, but not so high as to kill him and stop his breathing, just paralyse him. It was all part of his incredibly clever plan. David knew that Allan's partner, Kevin, wasn't going over that evening – Allan had kindly supplied that information. It had given David time to enact the next part of his perfect plan.

David had fetched a wheelbarrow from the garage and hoisted Allan into it. He was conscious, and wide-eyed. David wasn't the best at being able to understand people's emotions, but he'd been amazed by how much Allan's eyes seemed to convey what he'd presumed was fear. Before putting Allan into his own car, David had put on a pair of the thin rubber gloves that Allan used for dirty jobs. He'd seen the crime scene investigators on TV put these on and he didn't want them knowing that he'd been in Allan's car. He'd covered the driver's seat with a piece of plastic from the garage, and lay Allan along the back seat, being careful to put him on top of some tarpaulin to prevent anything leaking from him onto the seat.

David didn't want the security camera on the gate to see his face and so he'd put Allan's baseball cap on. That had been his least favourite part of the evening. The second he'd arrived at his destination and he was sure it was all clear, he'd whipped the disgusting thing straight off and repaired the damage to his hair.

David had thought through whether when he flung Allan off the cliff, he wanted him to land on rocks or go straight into the sea. He knew, again from a crime series that he'd watched with Jackie, that if Allan was alive when he went in the sea, then he would get water in his lungs, and that was plan A. The tragic drowning of a man who'd got nothing in his life but a boring job as some rich woman's driver. But it wouldn't necessarily cover up the knife entry point, all depending on what kind of state his body was in when he was eventually found – if ever. Plan B was therefore his back-up plan, but also so much cleverer.

David had sent a text to Kevin from Allan's phone, a whining message that said he'd really like to see Kevin tonight as he was feeling upset. Then he'd thrown his phone over the cliff top.

It had been early evening and so why the little girl had been still out and about, he didn't know. David had just thrown Allan, his phone, and his dirty baseball cap over the edge, but didn't have time to watch what the sea did with his body once it had plummeted onto the wave-covered rocks below, because he heard a sound from behind. He'd spun round and saw the little girl, staring at him wide-eyed.

'What did you see?' David asked her.

His voice seemed to bring the girl out of her shock and she turned to run back the other way but slipped on the dry ground. David was upon her before she could get up.

'Now, you're not going to tell anyone, are you?' David hissed at her. 'Because if you do, the bogey man will come for you and I'll have to throw your body off the cliff too.'

He could feel the girl's breathing shallow and rapid as he held her skinny arms, staring into her face.

From behind them, further back down the path, a woman's voice called out, 'Laura, Laura, where are you? Come back here now?'

'Then I could also take your mother, or perhaps I'll take her first...' David said. 'Or maybe I should just pick you up right now and chuck you over to be done with it.'

As he said the last words, a young woman came rushing along the path, appearing from behind bushes and a granite rock.

'Laura,' she'd called out in shock when she saw the two of them.

David's face softened into a charming smile, with an added layer of concern as he turned to greet her.

'Oh thank goodness, this little girl needs a big hug. She tripped over and gave herself quite a fright.'

David had smiled at Laura and stepped back as her mother rushed over to comfort her.

'Are you alright? I told you not to run on ahead, it's so dangerous along here. You could have tripped and fallen over the edge.'

David winked at the girl as her mother brushed her down.

'Thank you for helping her,' she'd said to David.

'That's no problem. Do you have far to go? I can help you get home if you like? She seems a little shaken up.'

The young mother had turned back round to David and smiled gratefully at him. 'Thank you so much but we don't live far. We're just off La Route de la Hougue.'

'Ah I've got friends who live along there, house on the corner, can't quite remember the number,' David said. He'd glanced at her ring finger, found it empty and he hadn't missed the flirting look she'd given him.

'We're close by, the white house with the bay windows,' she'd replied, smiling at the handsome man in front of her.

So easy. David had given her one of his best smiles and held on to her gaze.

Laura's eyes grew wider.

'Well if you're absolutely sure that you don't need my help.' David turned and smiled at Laura, who hadn't taken her eyes off him. 'I'm sure this little one will be right as rain once she gets back home.'

David thought about the girl and her mother as he drove back home from Saskia's. They'd both witnessed him at the location, which was a potential issue. He'd parked Allan's car not far away and so when it was found, there might be public appeals for witnesses, but they'd be looking for an ugly older man with greying hair, not a handsome young black-haired guy. She wouldn't put two and two together and he definitely didn't think that Laura would talk, not now that David knew where they lived. He'd be fine. His plan was too clever and so he pushed them out of his mind. As he had told Sas, he did listen to her – there was no way he was losing everything, not when there was still so much to gain.

TEN

THURSDAY

After David left, Saskia had opened the bottle of Pinot Grigio in the fridge, and was about to pour a glass but then thought better of it. Instead she turned her laptop on and started researching the Noirmont bunkers. Batterie Lothringen was the only coastal artillery battery fully completed and operational during the Jersey occupation. The German Organisation Todt literally blasted into the granite headland to create the structure. They built a command bunker, a tower into the edge of the point to observe ships and aircraft at sea, and of course several gun placements. But what could this have to do with Paul Cabot?

She found Jerripedia, the island wiki, which had a whole load of Jersey family tree information on it. It said that the name was thought to originate from the cabot fish, which apparently has a head too large for its body, and most of them seemed to have been based in the parish of Trinity. But she found little of use until there was mention of Philippe in St Brelade. It was as Matthew Cabot had said, Philippe was praised by some islanders in the parish for efforts to help feed locals, despite the Germans trying to requisition most of the food, and he went on

to become Constable of the parish. Saskia knew that wasn't a
police officer role as the name might suggest – although he
would have been head of the honorary police in the parish – but
a civic head role. A bit like a mayor.

Paul's father, Helier Cabot, then inherited the farm, before
passing it on to Paul when he died in 2003. It was a bit late for
his brother to be angry at Paul inheriting everything twenty
years after the event, although it's possible that the resentment
could have festered for a while. Yet it still didn't explain the
bunkers, or why Philippe's painting was damaged. The broth-
erly dynamic couldn't be ignored.

She clicked on a YouTube video of Paul being interviewed
for the election campaign. There were the standard manifesto-
style answers, him coming out with well-practised patter about
how he wanted to protect the rural environment, but at the
same time understood that we need to do something about
providing more affordable starter homes for the young people of
Jersey. He talked about how he would work to find a solution to
the long-running debacle about where to build Jersey's new
hospital and re-purposing the leisure facilities up at Fort Regent
on the hill above St Helier, so that it worked for the community.
None of it gave her any greater insight into his character. Even
when the interviewer questioned him, he smoothly transitioned
back to pushing his manifesto pledges, avoiding any controver-
sies. He'd have made a good politician.

Saskia looked on Google Maps for the route that Paul
would have taken late last night. The satellite imagery could be
a little out of date, but there were clear dirt paths leading across
the headland to various sections of the battery. Portelet Inn and
the houses and apartments that overlooked the bay were also
not far away, but in the opposite direction. Did the killer simply
want to take Paul away from where anyone could hear them?
Was she trying to read too much into the bunker location?

Perhaps it had just been a convenient quiet spot where, in the dead of night, nobody would hear a gunshot.

She got up and paced around her cottage. It was dusk, the light was fading as the sun began to head to its western bed chamber, but it was a warm evening and with the clear skies it would be a moonlit night. On an impulse, Saskia let Bilbo out into the back garden, then grabbed the keys for her motorbike, a strong torch, and pulled her front door closed before pointing her bike in the direction of Paul Cabot's house. She wanted to experience the area under similar circumstances to when the murder had been committed. Visiting the bunker today had been useful but with police and forensics officers swarming all over the area, it bore no resemblance to the way it would have appeared last night.

The Cabot house was in darkness when she arrived. Vicky and Daniel would probably have stayed over at Matthew and Gill's for the night while the police forensic officers finished with their home. Saskia could see the lights of their house across the fields, and apart from a faint glow from further along the lane, that was the only house nearby. It was quiet here, just the odd last few song notes from birds settling down for the night, or the raucous call of a pheasant in the fields. She could just make out the sound of the sea as waves met the rocky cliff face.

A gunshot when all around was quiet would have sounded loud, but was it reason enough to trek over the fields to the bunkers? Perhaps they'd just gone for a walk to see the sun rise and an argument had broken out there by chance, but that didn't explain why the pistol was taken from the house and used. Admittedly they didn't yet have confirmation from Forensics that it had been used in Paul's murder, but Winter had seemed pretty certain. That would mean it was pre-meditated.

There was still some daylight, but shadows were pooling in recesses and rather than lose her footing and potentially sprain an ankle, she turned on her torch. Would Paul and his killer have had torches for their walk? Quite possibly not, especially if they'd been drinking. Alcohol lowers inhibitions and makes people more reckless. And was he walking to the bunkers under duress, or did he go with his killer voluntarily?

She walked down the dusty dirt path at the side of the fields. A rustling in the hedgerow caused her to swing her torch round to see what it was. Almost at once, she realised it sounded too small to be anything that was a threat to her, but it had made her jump. Being alone in the near dark in a strange place when you're thinking about murder, could have that effect. It was probably a rodent or a hedgehog – there weren't even any foxes in Jersey. For a brief moment she thought about Bilbo and her snug little cottage with the lights on, and wondered why she hadn't just stayed there.

It didn't take her long to walk through the fields, and then she was onto the open heath of the headland. Rabbit holes were the main danger here so she kept the torch on while she walked, although the moon was now quite bright. Halfway across the headland, she stopped. The view was stunning – it was almost as if she had been transported to another world. In front of her, the sea was black and white, lit up by a bright moon that had laid a silver path across its surface that shimmered in the waves like a mirage. To her right she could see the lights of the houses and apartments at Portelet, and to the left, the glow of the island's main town, St Helier, a sprawling orange mass pinpointed in the sea by the lights highlighting the battlements of Elizabeth Castle. She turned her torch off for a few moments and just listened and looked. A breeze straight off the sea carried the whispers of the waves, secrets borne across the ocean, maybe from Puerto Rico, New York, or Nova Scotia. But what secrets did the land hold? The bunkers that Saskia could see silhouetted against the moonlit sky had many stories to tell. Their walls were seeped in the misery of forced workers, the angst of war, and now a more modern trauma.

Saskia was used to analysing others to understand their behaviour and standing there on the dark headland, she analysed herself and the feeling of unease which curled around her insides. Violence was her constant companion. It walked with her every day in her job. Sat with its menacing grin as the prisoners she worked with recounted the stories of their crimes. It had skipped by her side when she was a child. At first, the shadow of her father, and then her own brother. But while she'd seen violence, heard about it, and occasionally experienced it, she'd never seen the end result like she had today. The utter finality, the emptiness, the promise of a life destroyed at someone else's hands.

Now death sat at the back of her mind, spider like, spinning a web. It made her more jumpy even when it was just a mouse in the hedgerow. The thought of entering the dark, stinking bunker made her want to turn and walk back home to the lights of her cottage and Bilbo's warm fur. But Saskia had always faced her worst fears, never turned away from them, and so she took a deep breath of the sea air, turned her torch back on and walked purposefully towards the angular man-made structures that rose out of the heathland.

Saskia had just reached the road that ran across to the car park, when the sound of a car's engine and its headlights appeared from behind. That was irritating. She'd wanted to be alone. If it was a car full of rowdy young people coming for an evening away from parents where they could drink and smoke, then it would ruin the ambience of the place. She stopped at the side of the road. She couldn't hear music, no thump thump of drum 'n' bass or whatever the latest name for modern music was, so perhaps it was just someone wanting to experience the headland at night. Maybe a romantic couple come to hold hands and look out over the sea, or perhaps it was the killer returning to the scene of his triumph. That was certainly not out of the question. The black spider in the back of her mind stretched its legs and Saskia reached subconsciously for her mobile phone.

She stepped away from the road. The bright headlights were blinding, especially as her eyes had grown accustomed to the gloom, and she couldn't see the car, let alone its occupants. Not until it drew up next to her.

'I thought it was you. What are you doing here at this time?' Winter had wound down his window and was looking at her, a concerned expression on his face.

The black spider scuttled away.

'Winter! I wanted to come and experience the place as it had been last night,' she said.

'You know it's quite remote out here and we have a killer on the loose, you really shouldn't do that on your own,' he replied.

She didn't admonish him this time for being overprotective. He had a good point.

'I've got my phone,' was all she could say in return.

'Let me just pull over.' He moved on a few yards and pulled the car over to the side.

'Not sure why I've pulled off the road. We've still got it sealed off and have signs along the footpaths asking people to stay away. Seems to be working. Present company excepted.' Winter smiled and raised an eyebrow at her as he got out of the car and came to stand next to her.

'Is that why you're here?' she asked.

'No. I wanted to come and do exactly what you're doing,' he said, looking deeply into her eyes.

She couldn't miss the connection between them, the way

their eyes were drawn to each other's. The fact even their thought processes seemed to work the same way.

'Great minds...' she said, pulling her eyes away from his. 'Actually, if I'm honest, I'm quite glad you turned up. It's kind of spooky here in the dark.' Winter's presence felt like a warm overcoat in winter, wrapping around her. 'I walked from the Cabot's house. It didn't take long, ten minutes or so.'

Winter looked across the heathland in the direction she'd come from. 'We had a team walk it earlier to check in case there was anything along the way, but they found nothing.'

'Any results from Forensics?'

'We should have the ballistics report back in the morning. If it's Paul's gun then that obviously gives us some clear directions to go in. Nothing else yet, although as you know there were blood traces in the sink. We're just waiting on DNA confirmation that it was Paul's.'

Saskia simply nodded, thinking.

'I'm a little suspicious of his campaign manager, Joshua Redpath. He stayed overnight and was a bit secretive when he called his wife. Definitely one for us to look at in more detail.'

'He ran the campaign for Paul, do you think Paul's success somehow backfired, and Joshua resented it?'

'Seems like a strange reaction, but who knows what their agreement was? Perhaps Paul reneged on a contract or something.'

'So you still disagree with DCI Sharpe about it being politically motivated?'

'I can't rule it out, but no evidence so far. I'll be speaking to one of Cabot's fiercest social media trolls tomorrow morning, if you'd like to join me for that?'

'Sure,' Saskia said and then looked away from him in thought. 'I agree with you, by the way. I don't think this is political.' She wanted Winter to know that the DCI's comments earlier that day didn't reflect her line of thinking. 'What kind of man was he?'

'Paul Cabot? I never met him personally. Obviously saw him being interviewed during the election campaign, and he used to write a column in the *JEP* for a while, but I don't yet have a feel for him as a person. Once the news has sunk in, I'm going to talk to family and friends tomorrow and see if we can get a better understanding of who he was. You're welcome to join me for that too?' Winter said, then added, 'Sorry, I know you've got your own job to do. I can always tell you about it afterwards.'

'No, I could spare a few hours tomorrow,' Saskia said. 'Not the whole day, but I can catch up with paperwork that I'd have done in the office in the evening.'

'If you're sure, I mean I don't want this to take over or anything.'

'I'm sure. After all, it's likely that I'll be getting whoever the killer is visiting La Moye in the hopefully not too distant future, so it would be good to get a feel for who they are.' She smiled reassuringly at him.

Winter nodded in thanks, then they moved off towards the bunker that held their crime scene in silence.

Neither of them said a word as they stood and reviewed the pitch-dark bunker. It had been sealed off with police *No Entry* tape and they didn't break it. Although Forensics had finished, they erred on the side of caution. They didn't need to go right inside, and Saskia certainly wasn't in a rush to get back in there. Down between the concrete walls of the corridor that led to the bunker, it was even quieter. Despite it being open-topped, the sounds of the sea were silenced and every footstep became magnified.

'I know that common sense would say they came here where the gun shot might not be heard, but I don't think that was the only reason. Why do it execution style? Why not just shoot him wherever and get on with it if it was a crime of passion? This all has to have some meaning to the killer,' Saskia almost whispered in the dead of the night.

'You're still thinking it's someone he knew?'

'Definitely. They couldn't look at his face when they did it. Quite possibly he came voluntarily here. Sure, it might have been under duress with the gun pointing at him, but his clothes didn't look dusty or dirty. You'd have thought at some point in that walk across the fields, he would have tried to escape. To me that indicates he may have either been very fond of his killer, or trusted them.'

'Which again points to family or a friend. Be interesting to see what the pathologist tells us tomorrow, if there's anything that we couldn't immediately see.'

'That gun is also key.'

'Yes. Is there anything else you can tell us about what kind of person did this?' Winter asked hopefully.

'I need to know more about Paul and his family, but I strongly feel it's something very personal to them.'

'But why on election night? If it's not politically motivated, why then?'

'Perhaps seeing Paul win the election was the last straw, some kind of trigger in an already strained relationship, or perhaps the fact it was election night has nothing to do with the killer's reasons. It was just an opportune time.'

'Certainly gives us several potential suspects,' Winter replied, looking into the distance thoughtfully. 'Well, I guess there's not much more we can do tonight. I'll drive you back to the farm, did you come on your bike?'

'Yes, thanks.' The thought of walking back alone across the headland after being in Winter's presence, brought back a shiver of unease. As she got into the passenger seat of Winter's car and sat next to him for the short ride to the Cabot house, there was another feeling of unease. Being with Winter was so comfortable, like one of those soft fleecy blankets that you want to burrow into. They even thought alike. With every moment they were together she could feel a little molecule of the barrier she put up, dissolving away. She couldn't risk having a relationship with anyone, let alone a police officer. She couldn't risk her brother's freedom, and she certainly didn't want to risk Winter's life.

ELEVEN

THURSDAY

Despite the day he'd had, and the seriousness of the case, Winter couldn't help driving home with a smile on his face. Saskia had that effect on him. When his car headlights had illuminated her on the headland, his stomach had flipped. He'd not felt like this about a woman in a long time, if ever. Trouble was, it was clear she didn't feel the same way and yet he couldn't stop the fluttering in his stomach, or the longing. Admittedly, some of the fluttering might be to do with the fact he was hungry. He'd not stopped all day and besides a quick sandwich at lunch time, he'd not eaten. As soon as he got into his flat he went to the fridge, the vision of the bowl of spaghetti Bolognese that his mother had given him floating in his mind and making his tastebuds weep.

Winter had been at his parents yesterday evening. They'd called to ask if he could go over after work to help out in the garden. His parents were reasonably fit, but manhandling the lawnmower and cutting back some of the bushes that had grown like triffids around the flower beds, made their shoulders ache. 'Why put ourselves through pain when we have a strong, fit helper to call on,' his mother had said. He also knew there was an ulterior motive – she was always complaining that they didn't see enough of him and so this was partially an excuse to get him round.

'I can only stay for a couple of hours,' he'd told her. 'Got to go to Krav Maga after.'

She'd mumbled a reply, but accepted.

When he'd got there, his mother was cooking. 'I'll do you a portion,' she had said to him.

'Thanks, but I won't be able to eat it until after I've been to Krav Maga, Mum, remember?'

'That's alright, I'll give you a doggy bag to take home.' She still thought he didn't eat properly on his own.

He and his father had worked in the garden together while his mother popped in and out. He trimmed back a bush that had started to encroach on the dining room window, and he mowed the lawn. It was an old lawn mower and his father had wandered to and fro, collecting the cut grass and putting it into an old bin that he used for green waste.

'You know you can get one of those automated lawnmowers that will do this for you,' Winter said to him.

'What do you mean?'

'You know like a robotic lawnmower.'

'Oh what would we need one of those for, it's not that much trouble doing it ourselves.'

Winter didn't miss the irony of the fact it was always him they called to do it. He thought he might investigate a robot lawnmower for their Christmas present this year.

'Did you hear that Julie Jones, who's now of course a Denton, has just had twins?' His mother had come out of the house to watch them.

'Julie Jones? I didn't even know she'd got married,' Winter replied, a memory of a skinny freckled girl in Beaulieu Convent School uniform in his mind. 'Haven't seen her in ages.'

'She lives out in Rozel now, you know. One of those new glass things, I just don't think I would feel comfortable with all those big windows.'

'Probably got a great view,' Winter returned. He knew his mother had once had high hopes that he and Julie would get together. His mother got on well with Julie's mother. He also knew that his mum's updates on the marital and parenting status of his old school friends and peers was a little reminder that he ought to start thinking about it too.

'Mmmh,' his mother had said, disappearing back into the kitchen to stir something.

'She's cooking one of your favourites, you know,' his father said to him. 'Spaghetti Bolognese.'

Winter smiled, but hoped that she'd remembered he couldn't stay for dinner.

A little while later, he'd gone into the kitchen to wash his hands. His mother was trying to get a pan out of the cupboard. 'Let me get that, which one was it you wanted?'

'The big one for spaghetti.' She'd smiled adoringly at him. 'Cupboard door won't open properly anymore. Makes it so awkward.'

Winter got the pan out and then crouched down and looked inside the cupboard. 'It's the hinge. Didn't Dad have some spares of these in the shed?'

'Oh I don't know, love, can you ask him?'

Ten minutes later, Winter had a packet of hinges, already opened, and a screwdriver. Another ten minutes later he had the door off and was fitting the new hinge. He looked at the time.

'I'm going to have to go after this,' he said to her.

'Can't you stay for dinner, love?' she asked hopefully.

'Mum, you know I said I had to go and couldn't.'

'You're always so busy these days. Have you remembered to vote in the election?' she asked.

'Yes, did it first thing,' he reassured her.

She smiled. 'I'll get that glass Tupperware and fill it up for you. You can have it later.'

After he'd left his parents, Winter had gone on to his Krav Maga class. His was the intermediate level. He'd discovered the Israeli self-defence martial art a few years back and loved it for its practicalities. It was street fighting, learning to defend yourself from knife attacks, punches and gun attacks. Tonight they were working on thrust defences. He'd been taught self-defence as part of his police training, of course, but this was more intense, more raw.

For two hours he had lashed out at his sparring partner, or countered his attacks. He'd warmed up his shoulder muscles with the lawn mowing, and now he worked them and his arms hard. There'd been times in the past when he'd have liked to have bashed some of the criminals they'd had to deal with, but he knew that was both unprofessional and career-limiting. The gym was hot, unable to counter the summer air, and even in shorts and a T-shirt he'd been sweating hard.

'Fancy a beer?' His spar partner, Crispin, had asked as they were putting away the kit.

The thought of the cold liquid trickling down his throat was too much of a temptation – besides he only had an empty flat to go home to, and so he'd stayed. One thing led to another and he'd ended up getting some food too.

Some time later that night, when Winter had gone home to sleep off the beer and dinner, Paul Cabot was murdered.

What it meant was that when he came home the next day after the long day working on the murder case, he thankfully still had his mother's spaghetti Bolognese in the fridge waiting for him. He heated it up and collapsed in front of the TV to see what the local news were making of the investigation. Only, his mind wandered and he ended up thinking about Saskia, trying to imagine what she might be doing and eating.

TWELVE

FRIDAY

David was standing at the coffee machine, waiting for his double espresso to trickle out of the nozzle and into his cup. He liked the kick of the black coffee, the brief buzz as the caffeine hit his head. There had been times in the past when he'd dabbled in some harder drugs, in his misspent youth. He'd craved the feeling of excitement and euphoria that amphetamines had given him, but predictably they'd got him into trouble. That was when Saskia had stepped in. He'd not found it hard to stop the drugs, which his sister told him was because his brain was wired differently, but he did occasionally miss the high. Nowadays though, he preferred being in control. Allan had provided him with an alternative form of euphoria, a superior thrill, but that was fading.

A colleague, Alastair, wandered over to the kitchen. He'd just finished a can of ginger beer and there were strict recycling rules in their office, so he brought it over to the aluminium can bin in the kitchen, rather than dump it in the waste basket by his desk. There was some office push to buy trees for monkeys or something – one of the Durrell Zoo campaigns – and so bright animal pictures had been pasted onto the bin. David never took any notice of the latest corporate social responsibility campaign. They were all just crap attempts to make the firm look good anyway. Just like the ridiculous wellness schemes they introduced. They'd graduated from a fruit bowl and walking meetings, to mindfulness and encouraging people to share their worries over lunch. David had gone to a couple of sessions, purely for research. They turned out to be a goldmine for finding weaknesses in any colleagues he needed to lean on.

'Alright?' Alastair said to David as he passed.

David had still not found out who in the office had told his boss that he'd been trying to persuade clients to put more money into their hedge fund investments. As if David didn't know what he was doing! They could afford it and while they might well lose some, they also stood to gain more. Alastair was one of those he suspected might be responsible.

As Alastair wandered back to his desk, Nina, who was the recycling she-devil of the office, was heading to the kitchen herself. David quickly opened the recycling bin, took Alastair's can out and put it into the waste bin. Then he walked back to his own desk and listened with some pleasure to Nina's outrage as she went to put her teabag in the bin and found Alastair's can.

'Alastair! There's a ginger beer can in the bin, was that you? You're now fined one pound.' Everyone knew Alastair was the ginger beer fan and so Nina picked up the charity jar that was on the counter and shook it at him.

'But I put it in recycling,' Alastair had replied, rushing over to see the evidence. 'I swear I did.'

It was a small moment of amusement, but it satisfied David.

The only other opportunity to liven up his working day was to go and visit Cassie. She was the head of HR and David's current lust target. Married with kids, she was low risk for any repercussions, but would be a tough seduction, even with his good looks and charm. He'd provided himself with an 'in' giving her an expensive Lego kit for her twins which he'd told her had been won in a raffle to raise money for Teenage Cancer Trust in honour of a friend's son who'd died. She'd fallen for it, but he needed to do some more work. He'd yet to get an update on how the Lego building was going, so that was an opportunity to do some more charming.

David was just about to head to Cassie's office when his mobile rang. It was Jackie. He thought about ignoring it, but she rarely rang him at work, so it might be something interesting.

'Hi, darling,' he schmoozed.

There was a sniffing sound. 'David, they've found Allan's car at the top of some cliffs on the north coast. They think he's gone over.'

David had his response practised and ready. He even did the facial expression, although he knew she couldn't see. 'Oh my god, really? Are they sure? Do we need to go and search for him? He could be injured somewhere'.

'They've got people looking now, but someone reported that the car had been there at least two days and so the police are thinking the worst. Can you come home?'

'Of course, baby, I'm on my way.' David smiled congratulatorily to himself. All as planned – and he'd even get the rest of the day off work.

He sent an email to his boss, Steven Wood, and cc'd Cassie in, telling them that he had to leave to help with the search for a missing friend. After being the hero by saving the French client the other week when he'd had a reaction to the prawns in his sandwich, David was working on building up that image with Cassie. His next step would be to persuade her that Jackie was a nightmare and didn't love him, and that he needed affection. It usually worked, especially with the motherly types.

· · ·

When David arrived home, the gates were open and there was a police car parked in front of the house. Allan's flat door above the garage was also open and he suspected the police were searching for a suicide note or some evidence.

'Jackie!' David called out into the house.

'In here,' she'd replied and he followed the sound of her voice to the more formal sitting room which they rarely used except for occasions like this. A uniformed police officer was sitting on the sofa with a cup of tea in front of her, talking to Jackie and making notes in a book.

'David.' Jackie reached out her hands to him and he walked over, taking them and giving her a hug and a kiss.

'Are you alright, darling?' he asked. She held on to him and so he extended his embrace, taking his cues from her.

When she looked up at him, she'd been crying. 'I'm just so shocked. He didn't seem like the suicidal type, did he?'

'Are you sure it is suicide? The car could have just broken down and he's OK somewhere?' David said that more to the police officer than to his girlfriend.

'We aren't sure about anything at this time,' the police officer came out with her carefully worded reply. 'All we know is that the car was reported two days ago to the parish and once the missing persons' case was opened by your wife, we investigated.'

Neither David nor Jackie bothered to correct her marriage assumption.

'Can we help look for him? He could be injured somewhere,' David continued with his concerned friend act.

'I understand your concern and wish to assist, Mr Slater, but we have qualified search and rescue teams out there now looking for Mr Hall and having lots of members of the public in the vicinity will only complicate matters and possibly also result in further injuries.'

'Yes of course,' David said, dropping his head and doing his best look of concern. He chose to again ignore her mistake in using Jackie's surname for him. Usually it would irritate the hell out of him, having somebody not use his correct name, but it served a purpose today.

'Tell Sergeant Staples what you heard,' Jackie said, urging him with her tear-filled eyes.

'Well, it may not be relevant...' David said, feigning reluctance.

'Anything you can tell us at this time might help us with our enquiries,' Sergeant Staples replied. As he'd suspected she would.

'Well, it was Friday night. I was home alone, just sitting in the garden actually, having a few beers. It had been a busy week at work and Jackie had left for the airport earlier that afternoon. I heard a raised voice coming from the area of Allan's flat. It was Allan and he was talking on the phone to his boyfriend. I didn't listen in, it wasn't my business, but he sounded upset. Afterwards I heard a car leave and then I think that Kevin came round later. I heard a car arrive and Allan's flat door opening and closing and it sounded like his car engine. Then he left again not long after.'

'What time was this?' Sergeant Staples had her pen poised, making notes.

'I'm not one hundred per cent exact on the timings because, you know, I was chilling and not clock-watching, but the argument was before I ate, so probably about sixish. I then cooked myself some burgers on the barbecue and got through two beers, but the sun was still up, so I'd say Allan's car leaving was about seven-thirty. And Kevin coming round, more like nine to nine-thirty. But you know, it's not to get anyone into any trouble or anything. I've no reason to think that Kevin had something to do with why Allan isn't here.'

'No, no, of course not. This is a missing person's inquiry at this stage, so we're just gathering information. Thank you, both of you, and if anything else comes to mind, please get in touch.'

'We will, thank you,' Jackie said, moving as if to get up to show her out.

'You stay here, darling, I'll see the sergeant out,' David said, smiling at her.

He walked the police officer to the door. 'Please do let us know when you find him, won't you? I'm sure he wouldn't have taken his own life, he must have had an accident or something.'

The police officer looked at David sympathetically. 'Let's hope we find him safe and well,' she replied, but he could tell she didn't believe that.

Once he'd closed the door on her, he allowed himself a little grin before returning to Jackie.

'Are you OK, darling? Can I get you anything?'

'Thank you for coming back from work.' She looked up at him. 'I'm just so worried.'

'I know I didn't know him as well as you, but he didn't strike me as the suicidal type, although they do say that often it's difficult to spot.' David sat down next to her.

She nodded and leant into him, sighing with a little shiver.

'I have to say that I quite liked the sound of "your wife", when the police office said it,' he ventured. He hoped it wasn't too early to start the conversation, and that her vulnerability over Allan would make her more receptive.

'Mr Slater though.' She raised her eyebrows playfully at him.

'Yes, well, we could negotiate that.' He smiled back at her, giving her a kiss. The door was opened, now he could start the next stage of his plan.

THIRTEEN

FRIDAY

Winter had fallen asleep in front of the television, before waking himself up with a cricked neck. He rubbed it out and then finished off his sleeping in bed, ready for the six thirty a.m. alarm call. He woke up, mind instantly buzzing about the case. Would Forensics have any interesting results for him today, and would the pathologist reveal anything that hadn't been immediately obvious to them? He was also going to talk in more depth to Vicky Cabot and the other guests from election night. If there were no indications on the clothing they'd taken from everyone, then he would have to widen the net of suspicion. Unless, of course, one of them had been very smart.

He headed into the office to touch base with the team, but was soon back out and heading into town for a breakfast appointment with Paul Cabot's social media manager, Alfie Chen. Alfie had requested that they meet before he started work at the PR and marketing agency which was his day job. They arranged to meet in the Costa at the top of the main shopping area. Winter had checked out LinkedIn before setting off to ensure he knew exactly who he was looking for.

Alfie Chen was in his mid-twenties and surprisingly

nervous. He was there waiting outside for Winter and asked if they could sit inside, out of the way. It was obvious he didn't want people seeing who he was talking to. Winter would have preferred one of the outside chairs in the summer weather, but agreed and bought himself a white Americano, and Alfie a cappuccino with almond milk. He was a good-looking young man, mixed-race and fashionably dressed. As Winter ordered the coffees, he glanced over at him. There were flashes of confidence in Alfie, especially when young women of his age came in – he was aware of his looks and nice clothes, that was for sure – but the second that Winter sat down in front of him, all traces of that confidence evaporated.

Winter smiled reassuringly at him, keen to ensure he didn't clam up with nerves.

'Thanks for agreeing to see me. You obviously understand that we're investigating the death of Paul Cabot, and I've been told you were supporting him with his social media during the election campaign.'

Alfie nodded.

'How did you know Paul?'

'What do you mean?'

'I mean, how did you two meet?'

'It was Frank Mason who introduced us.'

Winter nodded, Frank had also been there on election night. He was a property developer, amongst other business interests. 'When was that?'

'Errr, about two months ago.'

'Two months ago! OK, So you hadn't known Paul until the election campaign was getting started?'

Alfie shook his head and looked away, avoiding Winter's eyes.

'You work in social media marketing, don't you?'

A nod.

'But it wasn't through the agency you work for?'

A head shake.

Winter was getting a grain of an idea as to why Alfie was being so cagey, but he thought he'd leave that question until a bit later. First, he'd get him onto firmer ground. 'So, tell me – was there anyone in particular who was trolling Paul online? Anyone who made any threats?'

Alfie visibly relaxed at the change in conversation away from himself.

'There were three in particular – Mary Roberts, Derek Page and Philip Jones, Derek was the worst of them, but I don't think Paul was particularly surprised or bothered by any of their comments. He didn't get any death threats – at least not on social media or via his website. Nothing that I saw anyways. But Derek turned up at a couple of the hustings and was a bit aggressive.'

'Aggressive?'

'Not physically like, but in his questions and the way he asked them. Tried to corner Paul at the end of one session to have a rant, but Paul dodged him.'

'You were there on election night? Did Derek Page turn up then?'

'Yeah, I was tweeting and using Insta and Facebook to keep people updated and make sure we got the right messaging out when he won. I didn't see Derek though.'

'Do you have lots of photographs from that night?'

'Yeah, yeah, I do actually.' He shrugged, as though wondering why Winter would want the pictures.

'Any from the party after?'

'A few. There was a lot of hanging around and waiting for the results first. Pretty boring actually.'

'And after the result?'

'Champagne, and I did my bit.'

'How long did you stay?'

'About an hour after the result. It's not exactly my scene, know what I mean? Most of them are twice my age.'

'Did you notice any issues with any of the guests? Did anyone have any arguments; was Paul ever looking annoyed or upset about anything?'

Alfie looked away from Winter and sipped at his cappuccino. 'Don't think so.'

The smell of evasiveness was stronger than the aroma of coffee.

'Alfie, it's important that you tell me everything. This is a murder inquiry and it's quite possible that somebody who was there that night killed Paul.'

'Not me!' he suddenly said in a panic. 'He was fine when I left.'

Winter decided to use Alfie's self-preservation mode to his own advantage. 'Everyone is a suspect at present, but I think you *did* see something, right?'

'I kind of just sat down and watched them all, like I said they weren't my crowd. There were a few things maybe...'

Winter waited. 'A few?'

'So, his son got right stroppy at one point. Paul had to go out the room and talk to him. I've no idea what it was about, but afterwards Paul spoke to Frank and then Frank got pissed off and left. That was all after the results. But Joshua the campaign manager – he was in a funny mood all evening. I thought he'd be all happy and celebrating, but he wasn't, not really.'

'Did anyone go into Paul's office and cause any damage?'

Alfie looked nonplussed. 'I wasn't following them around, I stayed in the lounge mostly.'

'Do you know why Frank Mason was annoyed?'

He looked away again and shook his head.

'What about the other guests? George Sanchez and Tom Le Feuvre?'

Alfie smiled. 'George got quite bladdered early on and fell

asleep for a bit. Tom was just there talking to everyone – he seemed to know Paul's brother and wife well too.'

'So you say that Joshua was in a funny mood, did he seem annoyed with Paul?'

'Mmmhh yeah, I'd say so. I don't know him well like, but I'd seen them both a couple of times for meetings and he was usually a bit of a suck up, you know? On election night he just seemed like he wasn't interested.'

'You said that they weren't really your crowd, so why were you helping Paul?'

Alfie squirmed a little and said nothing. Winter decided to help him out.

'Was Frank Mason paying for your time?'

Alfie looked a little panicky. 'It isn't illegal, I'm going to declare it on my tax. It's just a bit of freelance work.'

'I'm sure, but I suspect that Paul Cabot wasn't planning to declare it on his election expenses, was he?'

'Frank said it was just between us. I don't know anything about election expenses. Really. I don't want to get into any trouble.'

'It's academic now anyway,' Winter reassured him. 'But be aware of the rules in future. Is there anything else you can remember from that night? Anything that struck you as odd? How was Paul?'

'He was on good form, thought he was going to win and did, even got out some ancient family port which apparently they only ever drink at really important occasions. Only time I saw him on a downer was when he was talking to Daniel and then Frank, but he was fine after that.'

'Have you spoken to Frank since?'

Alfie shook his head. 'Wasn't expecting to really.'

'Would you mind sharing the photographs from that night with me please?'

'Sure, you got Bluetooth on?'

They both got their phones out.

'Most of the photos are a bit boring,' Alfie deftly sent a stream of images to Winter's phone.

'That's fine, one of them could hold a clue to find Paul's killer.'

'OK, that's all of them. From the parish hall and at the party.' Alfie looked back up at Winter's face, a look of relief at an imminent escape on his face. 'I really have to go to work now.'

'Thank you for your time and honesty,' Winter said to him.

Alfie got up to go and then paused. 'If you could not tell Frank that I dumped him in it, I'd appreciate it.'

'It's OK, I'm sure he understands that with a murder inquiry we will be finding out all sorts of information.'

Alfie nodded and left. Winter wondered what reason Frank might have to pay for social media help for Paul. The man never did anything that didn't result in some kind of gain for himself. Bribery, no matter how subtle, was an interesting motive.

FOURTEEN
FRIDAY

Winter would have liked to talk to Frank straight away, but the man was in a meeting all morning and not available until after lunchtime. Frank was a well-known figure in Jersey. A businessman who had his fingers in many different pies over the years, from restaurants and night clubs, to property development and office rentals. He'd mellowed a bit with age, the flamboyance giving way to a more mature style, and, from what Winter could tell, behaviour. But Alfie said that Frank had left the party after words with Paul; could whatever they had discussed been enough to make Frank return and kill him? Was Frank Mason capable of murder?

They'd managed to secure the clothing of everyone who stayed overnight at the house – there was no way that the killer could have escaped without some evidence on their clothes – but what if they had left and come back? Forensic officers were searching the Cabot household to ensure that nothing else had been worn and then discarded somewhere. But, if the killer had changed and then taken the blood-stained clothing with them, there was going to be no way to trace it. The blood traces in the sink were potential evidence that their killer had returned to the house after the murder, and, as soon as it was confirmed as Paul's blood, then it would be a certainty. Who would have the audacity to do that unless it was someone who could explain their presence in the house?

Winter knew that the external suspects also had to be looked at closely, and what Alfie had said about Derek Page couldn't be ignored.

Winter returned to the station just as Saskia was about to enter the building.

'Morning,' he said to her back, surprising her.

Saskia spun round and immediately rewarded him with a big smile. 'Morning.'

'We might as well head straight out as we're both here,' he said. 'Forensics have finished at the house so Vicky is going to meet us there later, but first port of call is Derek Page. He's well known for his online trolling and seems to have had a particular distaste for Paul.'

'I take it no forensic results yet?'

'Nothing yet. I'm hoping by midday we might have something on the gun, the clothes, and the blood in the sink. Also autopsy preliminaries. Just had an interesting conversation with Alfie, the young guy who was running Paul's social media campaign. He was being paid by the businessman, Frank Mason. That in itself is illegal as it should have been declared on election expenses, but, more interestingly, he witnessed an argument between Paul and his son, Daniel, and also with Frank himself.'

'Frank didn't stay overnight though, did he?'

'He didn't, but he could have come back and his presence there wouldn't have been particularly questioned as he was a supporter and had been there earlier. We need to find out if Vicky knows anything about it.'

'Or Daniel,' Saskia added. 'There were two arguments, they might be linked.'

Winter and Saskia made the short drive to the Le Marais tower blocks in St Clement.

'We have a long history with Mr Page,' Winter explained to Saskia en route. 'He has had a string of warnings, mostly for online abuse of politicians and other public figures in the island. He's on dodgy ground right now. One more wrong step and he could find himself with another custodial sentence.'

'Always good to check out my prospective clients ahead of time then.' Saskia chuckled.

'Well, I'm hoping you might be a slightly calming influence in the discussion. He doesn't exactly see eye-to-eye with the police, including me, but tends to be a bit more respectful around women.'

They'd arrived at the tall white Le Marais blocks which had been built in the early 1970s as social housing, with some significant refurbishments in more recent years. Some locals viewed them as an eyesore on the landscape because they could be seen from quite a distance across the otherwise low-level–built environment, but the community that lived on the estate was close knit and defensive of their homes. Those on the seaward side certainly had views that other people would pay a small fortune for.

Winter wasn't looking forward to talking with Derek Page. He'd had the misfortune of speaking to him a couple of years prior and had received a torrent of swear words and vitriol back then. A few years older, and Derek seemed to have got worse rather than mellowed. Some short-sighted individual had shown him how to get online and onto social media, and that had given him a public platform on which to share his views. Probably somebody with the best intentions at one of those silver surfer sessions, trying to get the older generation online. Derek had ended up serving a couple of months up at La Moye for racist comments. Now he sailed as close to the wind as he could with his abuse, and had discovered he could create additional accounts and anonymous personas to hide behind if required. Winter was all for free speech. Everyone had a right to air their views as long as they didn't hurt anyone, but these weren't views, they were personally targeted abuse.

Derek Page treated his working-class status as though it were a disability. Everything that happened in life to him was because he was working class, everything that he couldn't do or achieve was because he was working class. Every time someone didn't agree with him, it was because he was working class. There were without doubt big inequalities in Jersey, but in Winter's view, Derek Page wasn't a victim of his status in society, he was quite simply an unsavoury personality who very few wanted to spend time with. His isolation was down to who he was, not what he was.

Derek Page opened the door to Winter and Saskia, then immediately tried to shut it again. Winter had been ready for that move and had his foot and shoulder in position. Experience had taught him that you needed both in order not to have one or the other take the brunt of a slamming door.

'You can't do that. Where's your warrant?' Page snarled at him, and peppered his question with a few choice swear words.

'I can come back with a warrant and have you down at the station to talk if you'd prefer, or we can just have a quick chat here in the comfort of your own home. Which will it be?' Winter saw the dilemma on Page's face and stepped back so that if he still wanted to close the door he could. He didn't.

'Wot's it about?'

'If you don't mind inviting us in then I can tell you, rather than discuss it here where your neighbours can join in.' Winter gave his best congenial smile. 'This is Saskia Monet, a forensic psychologist.'

'Wot, you're trying to make out I'm nuts now, are you?' Page looked Saskia up and down.

'Not at all, Mr Page. I'm just helping DI Labey with an ongoing investigation. I'm not here to clinically assess your mental health. This is my first time in these flats – you must have a fantastic view.'

Winter recognised Saskia's calming professional voice.

Derek narrowed his eyes at her, clearing considering his next move.

'Five minutes and if you try it on, I'm calling my lawyer,' he eventually replied, opening the door to them both and instantly walking inside his flat expecting them to follow. He was limping slightly and Winter could see what looked like a bandage underneath his right trouser leg.

'You're perfectly at liberty to call your lawyer now if you'd prefer,' Winter said to his back, knowing full well that he wouldn't. Lawyers cost money.

Page slumped himself down onto an old armchair, stained with countless TV dinners, spilt beer, and general grease and dirt. Winter would have preferred to stand rather than sit on the sofa, opposite. He could determine that on one side someone had spilt a curry at some point. While there was no way of telling what kind of curry it had been – all lumps and residue long since wiped away, there was still the yellow staining from the turmeric in the sauce. He did the gentlemanly thing and chose the seat that looked the muckiest, leaving the other for Saskia.

The flat reeked of stale cigarette smoke which had also done its part in giving a yellow stain to the wallpaper, and a jaundiced feel to the whole place. Piles of old *Jersey Evening Post* newspapers and a fair few copies of the *Sun*, were scattered around. There was a dining table with two chairs against the wall but Page clearly preferred to eat in front of the TV, judging by the two plates with dried remains piled up on the small table beside his seat, and the fact the dining table was covered in paperwork, discarded carrier bags, a dead-looking plant that Winter couldn't identify, and a used mug.

Page's circumstances didn't make him a bigot – Winter had dealt with some seemingly highly respectable members of Jersey society in the past who had expressed less than diverse views and voiced them to individuals – but the state of his flat did reflect something of the man himself. Page was as dirty and dishevelled-looking as his home.

'You hurt your leg?' Winter asked him to try and make conversation.

'Na bloody cellulitis, damned pain, can't get to the pub as often as I'd like. Family Nursing come and sort it.'

Winter nodded. 'I want to be quick and not waste your time or mine,' he said to him, laying down his expectations upfront. 'You've been close to the line in some of your election commentary...'

'But I've not said anything that would break the law,' Page said smugly.

'No. But there's been an incident and I need to know where you were yesterday evening.'

'An incident?' Page suddenly became interested. 'What kind of incident?'

Winter weighed up what he should say. 'I can't disclose that at present, but it involves Paul Cabot, who you have had several choice words to say about over the past few weeks.'

'Oh that entitled shit,' Page sneered. 'Makes out like he's a working man, a farmer, has to keep up the Jersey traditions and all that bullshit. He was handed the whole bloody lot by his father. Shafted the brother you know. Followed the old Jersey way and gave the whole lot to the eldest son so that it didn't get split up. Cabot's not done an honest day's work in his life. And he reckons he's representing Jersey people. Well he certainly don't represent no one I know. The man has no principles.'

'So, can you let me know where you were yesterday evening?'

Page analysed Winter for a few moments.

'Here. Listened to the results on Radio Jersey with a few beers.'

'Anyone verify that?'

'Nope, apart from a very nice young woman coming round from Family Nursing, I was home alone. On Twitter,' he added. 'That nosey old bitch upstairs banged on the floor about half twelve wanting me to turn the radio down.' Page glanced at Saskia as he said that.

'And you didn't leave at all?'

'No. Not exactly up for a jog round the block, am I?' He gesticulated at his leg and then turned to Saskia. 'You see! This is what I 'ave to put up with all the bleedin' time. Harassment, that's what it is. Why do you think I don't wanna talk to 'im?'

'I appreciate that we've disturbed your day, Mr Page, but I assure you that DI Labey is talking to lots of people and we are simply working for the best outcome for everyone.' Saskia smiled warmly at Derek. 'Have you lived in these flats long?'

'Ay. Been 'ere over twenty years now.'

'It really is a fantastic view,' she said, glancing out of the window. 'Have you always lived in the east of the island?'

'Yup, St Clement born and bred.'

'Good bus routes?' she asked.

Winter wasn't exactly sure where her line of questioning was heading but he let her continue.

'Yeah, pretty good as it happens. I go everywhere on the bus, got me free pass now see. Can't afford a car, bloody petrol's gone up so much. Used to be cheap here, now it's more expensive than the United Kingdom. Everything's gone up ridiculous in this island. Government is squeezing us dry. Keep putting up taxes on everything. Establishment favours its own, don't give a shite about people like me.' Page glared towards Winter who he clearly included as establishment.

'You said that Mr Cabot has no principles, what was it about Mr Cabot that you particularly disliked?'

Page looked at Winter again. 'Just don't like his bullshit, that's all.'

Winter waited but the look from Saskia said she'd like him to leave them alone for a moment.

'OK, well thank you for your time, Derek,' Winter said, standing. He highly doubted Page was their man, unless he was lying about the cellulitis, but that would be easy to verify and they could also check with the neighbour upstairs.

'That it?' Page looked at Saskia, almost disappointed. He clearly wasn't bothered about Winter leaving.

'Yes. Told you we'd be quick,' Winter said and started walking towards the front door.

'It really is a great view,' Saskia added, standing and looking out the window.

Winter was almost at the door, keen to get going and away from Page, but he also sensed that Saskia was on to something.

'You must see a lot from up here,' Saskia continued. 'Did you also see something that you didn't like about Paul Cabot?'

Page hmphed and dropped his voice slightly, as though he didn't want Winter hearing.

'Maybe. Maybe I *can* tell you something you don't know about that sly bugger, Cabot,' Page muttered. 'He ain't the upstanding citizen he makes out.'

Winter turned and watched them, but didn't say anything.

'He was having an affair. Preached about family values and all that shit, but he was having it away with someone on the side.'

There was a smug smile on Page's face.

'Bet Mr Big Shot Detective over there didn't know that!'

'Thank you, Mr Page.' Saskia pulled his focus back to her. 'How did you find that out?'

'Saw 'em after one of the Hustings. Thought no one was watching 'em.'

'Were they kissing?'

'They were kissing alright. He had his hands on her and all.'

'Do you know who she is?'

'Dunno. Some bird with blond hair. Maybe the detective could work that out.' Page smirked. 'Or maybe not.'

Winter pulled the door open and left without another word. He heard Saskia thanking Derek and following him out.

'Nice bloke, don't you think?' he said to her in the lift. He couldn't help it with Page, he rubbed him up the wrong way. Bigots were one of his pet hates.

'Not someone I'd choose to have a drink with, but I've met worse. I can see that things are a little frosty between you.'

'Frosty is one way of putting it. He's not our killer, not even sure that what he said about the affair is true. What do you think?'

'I think he believes it is. I detected that he was holding back on something earlier, probably didn't want to say it when you were asking the questions because he didn't want to help you.'

'Yeah, you're probably right,' Winter sighed thoughtfully. 'A good thing you came along then because if it is true, it could give us the motive we've been looking for.'

FIFTEEN

FRIDAY

Saskia and Winter drove through the tunnel and along the avenue, heading west. One lane each way was closed off as workers erected the banners and other decorations for the upcoming Battle of Flowers parade the following week. Others were delivering the metal stands in West Park which ran along the side of the road.

'I've never been to a Battle of Flowers,' Saskia said as much to herself as to him.

'Did you not go when you were little?'

'No, it wasn't my parents' thing and I wasn't even four when we left.'

'It's a fun event, real community feel as most of the parishes, as well as other organisations, put in floats. Definitely worth seeing.'

Winter thought about suggesting to Saskia that he could take her along, but two things stopped him. One was that she might think it was him asking her on a date, which if he was honest he'd like to do but didn't want to compromise their working relationship; and secondly, he might not be able to go if this inquiry was still ongoing. The first couple of weeks were always very busy with an investigation like this.

Winter had been to the Battle most years. The annual event was one of Europe's most spectacular flower carnivals. Themed floats decorated in fresh and dried flowers rode the length of the closed-off avenue and grandstands with eating and drinking areas ran along the sides. It was a really happy family event. When he'd been younger he'd also taken part, dressing up in costume and riding along on his parish float. His parents had helped with fundraising over the years in the parish, and his mother usually went along and volunteered to stick on flowers, just like his grandmothers had. There were plenty of photographs in the family albums. He'd been roped into helping with that too over the years. He'd moaned a bit as a teenager when it seemed uncool to be involved, but now he appreciated the event. There weren't many communities that came together like they did in Jersey to put on something that had been going for over a century – wartime excluded.

They arrived at the Cabot house and Winter's knock on the front door was answered by a flustered Vicky.

'There are things missing,' she said. 'We've been robbed.' Tears welled up in her eyes again and Winter felt for the woman. Bereaved and now violated by a thief.

They followed her into the house. 'What's gone missing and do you have any idea when they disappeared?'

She'd led them through to a dining room where a long wooden table with enough chairs for a dozen people dominated the centre of the room. Around the walls were a selection of antique dressers and cabinets.

'There were two antique silver inkwells on the mantle-piece,' she said pointing to an Edwardian fireplace that looked as though it was still used in winter. 'They were a beautiful pair, unusual. Paul said he'd had them valued once and they were worth about a thousand each.' She spun around, getting more aggravated now that she had an audience. 'And on the bookcase there, we had some first editions – they're gone. Look, you can see where someone has shoved the other books up so that it doesn't look as obvious.'

Winter peered at the bookcase, but Vicky had already moved on.

'Through here, in the sitting room, we had two Lalique vases. Gone.'

They reached the sitting room and Vicky, exasperated, had thrown her hands towards an empty spot on a dresser. Tour of the stolen goods over, she crumpled into a heap on the sofa.

'I'm so sorry, Mrs Cabot. We need to determine when these went missing and if it's in any way related to your husband's death. You didn't notice them gone yesterday?'

Vicky looked up at him, tears streaming down her face. 'No, but I wouldn't have. I'd not gone into the dining room yesterday morning before you came to tell me about Paul, and then we left the house. I spent most of my time in the kitchen.'

'Were the missing pieces family heirlooms or particularly important to Paul?' Saskia asked.

'I think he'd inherited them, they've just always been here,' she said to Saskia.

'And they were definitely here the night of the election?'

'Yes. At least I think so...'

'I have some photographs on my phone from that night. Nothing from the dining room but some of them were taken here in the sitting room,' Winter said, pulling his phone from his pocket.

He flicked through the images that Alfie had sent him. There were several which didn't have the right angle, but then one of Paul and Tom celebrating. Tom was raising a glass to Paul's, clearly congratulating him. The pair of them were smiling and laughing, and behind them Winter could see the two Lalique vases, clearly visible.

'The vases were here on the night of the party. Let me contact the team at the office and get them to check the photographs that Forensics took yesterday morning.'

Winter moved out of the sitting room and left Saskia and Vicky alone.

He dialled Jonno's number.

'I need you to check something for me with the photographs taken yesterday at the Cabot household. There are some items missing and we need to determine if they were taken the night of the murder or if somebody has gone in last night to help themselves knowing that the family weren't here.'

'OK, what you want me to look for?' Jonno was straight down to business.

'Sitting room, in particular to the right of the fireplace there's a wooden dresser. Can you see two glass vases on it?'

There was silence apart from a few clicks from Jonno's mouse.

'Dresser... nope. Nothing that looks like a glass vase. There's some china and photographs in silver frames, but nothing I'd call a glass vase.'

'Can you send that photograph through to me just to confirm we're both talking about the same dresser?'

'Sure, I'll do that now. Do you need me to get another team down there to help? How much has gone missing?'

'A few thousand pounds worth by the looks of it, but not so much that one person couldn't have carried it out themselves. If your photo confirms it, which it sounds like it will, then they went missing some time in the night or early morning of the murder which makes it quite possible that our killer had something to do with it. We won't find any other evidence in that case as Forensics have already been over the place after they were stolen. I'll get the family liaison to get a statement from Vicky detailing what's gone.'

'So this is a robbery gone wrong?'

'It's possible. Maybe the killer did just take Paul to the bunker to avoid waking the others and raising suspicions about the stolen goods too soon. Perhaps they planned to take more but Paul caught them.'

Before Winter went back into the sitting room, he waited for Jonno's photograph to come through to his phone. It was as he'd said. Same dresser minus the vases. They had no proof of when the items in the dining room were taken, but most probably it was the same time.

Winter returned to the sitting room in time to hear Saskia asking Vicky what kind of a man Paul had been. He sat down quietly, not interrupting.

'He wasn't perfect. But he was pretty generous to friends and family.'

'How long had you been married?'

'Twenty years in September.'

'And did you know each other before? You're from Jersey too aren't you?'

'Yes I am, but not really. Our paths hadn't crossed before, possibly because my family come from Rozel way and Paul went to boarding school in England. We met at a friend's wedding actually,' A faint smile curved Vicky's lips as she relived the moment. 'He was a bit drunk from what I remember, but him and Tom were funny. Bit of a dull wedding. They livened it up.' Her face dropped back into grieving.

'You must have lots of happy memories.'

Vicky nodded.

'Did you know Paul's father?'

'Yes, not for long because he died just after we were married, but it was nice that he got to come.'

'Is that when Paul inherited the house or did his mother stay here for a while?'

'Everything went to Paul, but he'd never have kicked his mother out you know. She offered to move into the dowager's cottage. It was just her and she said she hoped that we'd start a family.'

'And Matthew got the other farmhouse?'

'No actually, that's Paul's too but he lets his brother live there in return for looking after the land.'

'So when you said everything went to Paul, it really was everything?'

'Yes. I know what you're thinking, that seems unfair on Matthew, but it's the family's protection mechanism. If you start splitting the land and the wealth, then it's watered down and lost by the time you get to the grandchildren. By handing it to the first-born son, it gets kept together and retains its value.'

'Did Paul never sell any of the land?'

'Only some very small areas which were more trouble than they were worth.'

'Was Matthew never resentful about that?'

'He grew up with knowing that's what would happen so it wasn't a surprise or anything. I'm not going to lie and say there weren't occasional arguments between them. If Matthew needed something he'd come and ask Paul, sometimes they'd bicker, but they always made up. Paul was generous to him.'

'Has Paul continued the family tradition?'

'You mean does Daniel get to inherit everything?'

Saskia nodded.

'Yes, he does. I'm hoping he won't kick me out the house yet,' Vicky joked weakly.

'Surely Paul will have left you with some means?'

'We'll see, won't we? To be honest, we never really discussed it past the fact that Daniel would just automatically get everything when he died. I didn't expect him to die so soon...' Vicky trailed off.

'If you don't mind me asking, was everything OK between you both?'

Winter held his breath. He was glad that Saskia had asked that question and not him. It had somehow come across more gently, but then she was a psychologist and used to interviewing people and giving therapy.

Vicky looked away from them both and bit at her bottom lip to try to stop herself from crying again. For a moment she didn't seem to know what to do with herself or what to say.

'I suppose it is going to come out, that's if you don't know already,' she said, the latter remark aimed at Winter. 'On the night of the election, Joshua told me that Paul had been having an affair with his wife. I know she's not the first, but I did think he'd have grown out of it by now. Poor Joshua was devastated, not surprisingly. He'd just given up a great deal of time and effort to help get Paul elected.'

'How did that make you feel, Vicky?' Saskia's soft voice encouraged her on.

'Shitty, what would you expect?' She looked at Saskia defiantly, chin stuck out. 'He wouldn't have left me, I know that, but still, it's insulting.'

'Did Joshua talk to Paul about it?'

She shook her head. 'He said he wasn't going to, not that night, not until he'd decided what he and his wife were going to do first. But he'd wanted me to know.' Then she looked up, her eyes suddenly on fire. 'Oh my God, you don't think that Joshua killed Paul, do you? He slept here that night. I'd gone to bed.'

Winter stepped in. 'We have no evidence to suggest that, Mrs Cabot, there were several people who might have had the opportunity, or it could have been a random stranger. It's too early in the investigation to say yet but I can assure you that should we arrest a suspect, you will be the first to know.'

That seemed to placate her for a moment, although it was obviously a definite possibility. Winter had some questions too.

'Did you talk to Paul about it?'

She shook her head. 'They'd just got the family port from the cottage and were all making a fuss about it. I decided to go to bed at that point, couldn't stand all the celebrations.'

Winter thought for a few moments, logging all the information.

'Can I ask you about Frank Mason? Did you know him well?'

She shook her head. 'I can't say I did. He was a business associate of Paul's, started coming round about six months or so ago. Paul said he was talking to him about something that they were going to work on together. I didn't know what it was. I suppose I'm sounding like the vague wife, aren't I? I should have taken more notice, but Paul could be quite secretive. When you've been married as long as we have, you tend to have your own projects and friends if you want to retain any semblance of individuality. I'm not saying that those relationships where people live in each other's pockets all the time are wrong, it just wasn't for us. I like meeting up with my girlfriends and doing yoga or going to my book club. Paul certainly wasn't interested in yoga or reading books, but he had his business interests. God only knows how we're going to work out all that now. I suppose Daniel will have to take a year out before university and try to get on top of everything.'

'Apparently Paul said something to Frank last night and he got annoyed and left. Were you aware of that?'

'No, not at all, but to be honest, if it was later in the evening, which it must have been because Frank was there until after I'd gone to bed, then I wouldn't have known, or perhaps not cared after I'd spoken to Joshua. Frank seemed fine when I saw him.'

'And Paul seemed fine when you said goodnight?'

Vicky looked down at her lap and her face once again

creased into tears. 'I didn't,' she said, her voice barely a whisper. 'I didn't say goodnight to him because I was so annoyed about what Joshua had told me. I just went to bed and left them to it.'

Winter thought that the look on Vicky's face was the evidence of a guilt she would always carry with her, that despite the hurt he'd caused her, she'd never said goodbye. Or was this all just a show to hide the fact she'd killed her own husband in anger later on that night and, instead, the look of guilt and regret was that of a murderer?

SIXTEEN

FRIDAY

The conversation with Vicky had been quite illuminating. Saskia could see that Joshua Redpath was an obvious suspect, and clearly a favourite as the cuckolded spouse, and Vicky herself couldn't be discounted, and yet there were questions about Frank Mason which Winter was seriously considering. Plus, if she was a punter at the races, she'd say that the brother, Matthew, would also be on the betting slip, albeit with long odds.

'The stolen items have been carefully picked,' Winter said to her while they waited for Vicky to get Daniel so they could have a chat with him. 'There are plenty of things which look valuable to me, but I don't have a clue about antiques. It looks to me that the person who stole them, knew what they were taking. Joshua Redpath runs an antiques business.'

Saskia didn't have time to react to that piece of information because Daniel had sloped into the room.

'Hi, Daniel.' Winter immediately changed his tone of voice. 'Thank you for talking to us. I know it's not easy at this time, but there are just a few questions we'd like clarified as it can help us with the investigation.'

The boy nodded.

'What time did you stay up until on the election night?'

'Err, 'bout half one.'

'Was that around the same time as your mum?'

'She went up about one.'

'Was Frank Mason still there when you went to bed?'

Daniel's face twitched as though irritated. 'Yeah.'

'I have to ask you this as it's been mentioned by a witness. Did you have an argument with your dad on election night?'

'No. Why would I? He's my dad. He'd just won the election.'

Saskia was watching Daniel closely and although up until then she'd felt he was being honest with them, the last answer didn't ring true. His leg had immediately started to jiggle up and down and he clasped both his hands together, winding his fingers around each other as though seeking comfort and reassurance.

'Daniel, I'm not trying to upset you, I know how hard this is.'

'What, your dad's been murdered too?' Daniel shot back.

Winter looked a little chaste at the hurting young man in front of them. 'No, I meant that I've had to investigate murders like this and try to work to get answers for family members like you, before. I know how painful and how tough this time is and that you just want to know what happened to your dad. I'm trying to give you those answers, Daniel.'

'Frank Mason is a dick. He was trying to con my dad into selling this place so he could develop it and make a fortune. This is our home!' Daniel suddenly blurted out.

Saskia felt for the boy who was suddenly going to have to grow into a man with responsibilities overnight. He was angry and he was hurting.

'Did your mother know about this?' Winter asked.

Daniel shook his head. 'I asked my dad about it and he said he wasn't going to go through with it.'

'Who told you about it?'

'My uncle. He'd had quite a few drinks and as they were leaving, he told me then.'

'Did your dad speak to Frank after you?'

'I dunno. Maybe Dad told Frank he was deluded and that's why he got annoyed. He's not going to get near this place now. I'll make bloody sure of that.' Daniel seemed to realise that he'd sounded angry and was talking to a police officer. 'Mum said that some things have been stolen?' He changed the subject.

'Yes, it appears they went missing on the same night. Obviously we're trying to see if the two crimes are linked.'

'Right.'

Winter's mobile buzzed in his pocket and he excused himself and took the call. All Saskia could hear was him asking the caller *where*?

'Did Joshua Redpath seem OK to you on election night?' Saskia asked Daniel.

He shrugged. 'Fine. Bit quiet but he's not exactly the life of the party anyway.'

Winter rushed back into the room.

'I'm really sorry but something has come up that I need to deal with urgently.' Winter said it as much to Saskia as to Daniel. 'Daniel, thank you for your help. I will be back in touch very soon with any updates. Miss Monet, I'm going to get someone to take you where you need to be and I'll give you a call later if that's OK, as soon as I've dealt with this.'

Winter didn't wait for either of them to reply and was off and out the door, talking into his mobile again. Saskia wondered what could be so urgent that he dropped everything, including her, and had to leave. Had Forensics come up with some clear evidence?

'Did you talk to your dad in his study?' Saskia asked Daniel in Winter's wake.

'Yeah.'

'And the picture of your great-grandfather was still on the wall then?'

'Yeah, it was fine.'

'It's really important that you tell us if you saw that it wasn't because it could be a critical clue in this case.'

'I told you, it was fine, and I certainly didn't touch it. Why would I? I never knew him, but my gran used to talk about him all the time, and Dad, so I kind of felt like I did.'

'Do you think your dad would have agreed to walk across the fields to Noirmont?'

'What do you mean?'

'Well, would he have enjoyed looking at the sunrise perhaps?'

'Maybe. I dunno. I guess if one of his mates had suggested it. He was in a good mood.'

'Was he particularly interested in the occupation years?'

Daniel shrugged and screwed up his face. 'Just as much as anyone of his age is, you know. They'd always celebrate Liberation day and I'd hear the same stories about how my great-grandfather had tied their last horse to the cart and taken the family into St Helier for the celebrations but halfway there the cart had lost a wheel and so they'd just abandoned it and Great-grandma and her sister rode the horse bareback the rest of the way while everyone else walked. Forever hearing about how I should walk more and not expect a lift, or be grateful we've always got food cos they didn't have much.'

Saskia had a thought.

'Do you know if anyone else besides your uncle knew about Frank's plans for your house?'

Daniel looked at her. 'Why?'

'Because it might be important.'

'I don't know. It's not relevant. I've got to go now anyway.' The expression on his face challenged her to make him stay. She didn't.

It was obvious Daniel was trying to downplay the significance of finding out about the deal, but surely if he thought that his uncle or someone else had killed his father he'd be willing to give them the name? She'd bring it up with Winter later.

So much of this family revolved around the farm and the inheritance. Daniel was the one to benefit from his father's dying. If Paul had sold to Frank Mason, Daniel would have lost his family inheritance which gave him a motive. Matthew might have been angry that his brother was selling everything that he'd lost out on in order to preserve the family heritage. He'd also likely lose his rent-free home. The whole case seemed to revolve around their family and its history. Had that history come back to haunt them?

SEVENTEEN

FRIDAY

The phone call that DI Winter Labey had received was from the office to say that the body of a man, suspected as that of a convicted robber, had been found floating off the sea around St Catherine's breakwater. Knowing that items had been stolen from the Cabot household, and that generally speaking bodies didn't float until they'd been in the water a few days, they obviously had the prospect that the remains could be linked to their murder inquiry. He could easily have gone in off the north-west coast. The tide streams ran in different directions depending on the tidal times, but no body ever stayed in the same place it had originally gone in – not unless it had been weighted heavily.

The body of the man had been collected by the St Catherine's lifeboat crew, called out by a local fisherman. Winter headed straight there. From where he was in St Ouen, it was almost the opposite corner of the island and required him to head back towards St Helier. He put his lights on down the avenue where it was safe to go above the forty mile per hour maximum speed limit. This was the only road in Jersey with more than one lane in each direction. Locals joked that it was their motorway, although some took it a little too far and tried to do the speeds that you'd see on English or European motorways, and invariably ended up being attended to by police or ambulance.

Once he'd reached the outskirts of St Helier, Winter took the cross-country route, going round the back of St Helier and up the Five Oaks and Maufant way. It still took him over half an hour to reach the lifeboat station from where he could see the long arm of St Catherine's breakwater reaching out to protect the bay.

A team were there already and the body had been bagged ready for transportation.

'DI Labey,' one of the uniformed sergeants greeted him. 'We haven't had formal identification, but we believe it to be Allan Hall, forty-five, whose car was found parked near the cliffs on the north coast a few days ago. He served twelve years in England for armed robbery.'

'What's he doing over here?' Winter asked as they walked over to the body bag.

'He was born here, left when he was eighteen for England. Came back after his sentence and has been working as a driver for the property developer, Jackie Slater. She reported him missing and he was registered as a MisPer.'

'Anything on him?'

'No.'

'I appreciate he's been in the water a few days but any obvious signs of injuries apart from natural post mortem?'

'I tried to look, sir, but it's impossible to say.'

'And when exactly do we think he went missing?'

'Last text from him and sighting, was a week ago today.'

'Had he been depressed?'

'Not according to Ms Slater or his boyfriend, a Kevin Smith.'

'So on those timings, he should have been in the water a week?'

'Yes.'

'Does that correlate with body condition?'

'I'm really not a hundred per cent sure, sir.' The young officer looked a bit green around the gills and Winter could tell he was hoping that he wasn't going to have to take another look.

'OK thanks, I'll take a look.' Winter was no expert but he'd a reasonable idea from having seen previous drowning cases, of what state he'd expect to find Allan Hall's remains in. From what the officer was saying, it was unlikely that this was related to his murder case. Allan had already been missing for several days before Paul Cabot was killed, but it was still worth double-checking.

Quite apart from the stench, just a quick look inside the body bag confirmed the likelihood that Allan Hall had been dead longer than just since Wednesday night, or early Thursday morning. The case would still need to be investigated – who was to say that it was suicide. But for now, Winter could park this one as separate to his current inquiry, until the pathologist had the opportunity to file his report, and then he'd see if any further action was needed.

It was a relief of some sorts, even if a robbery gone wrong might have been a more convenient motive for Paul Cabot's murder.

Winter thanked the lifeboat crew and the uniformed officers, and walked back to his car. He allowed himself a few moments to get over the experience of looking at the body bag contents. He'd long ago accepted that he wasn't made of granite like his island, and that there were some sights, smells, and experiences that had an impact on him. Just thinking about mental health brought a far more pleasant image into his head of Saskia Monet. It was almost like taking a sorbet palate cleanser in-between courses.

Winter stared out at the bay in front of him. France was just across the water, a dark band stretching out as far as he could see on top of the aqua blue water. To his left the breakwater and to his right the Martello tower at Archirondel, stood out on the rocks, blocking any view further round the coast to Gorey. A flashback of sailing in little dinghies came to him. He must have been twelve or thirteen, and his parents had paid for a sailing course in the summer holidays. Him and Jonno, plus another one of their friends, Greg, had all done it together. Two weeks on the water, with some classroom learning, not a care in the world except whether they'd get time to sail across the bay to get an ice cream at the Archirondel café, or instead have to wait until after the lessons and walk up to the café near to St Catherine's breakwater. Such big dilemmas. He'd enjoyed the sailing, but it wasn't until his parents had let him do the surfing course the following year, that he found his true love.

Mind cleared, Winter pulled his mobile out and looked at the time. He was due to see Frank Mason in just over an hour. He dialled Saskia's number to see where she was and if she wanted to join him.

'Apologies for disappearing off, they'd pulled a body from the sea and I needed to check if it was related to our case.'

'It's fine, I carried on chatting to Daniel. He seems cagey about the Frank Mason deal.'

'Protecting someone maybe?'

'Maybe, could be the brother? He had a lot to lose if Paul sold the whole place, not least his house and his livelihood, but so too did Daniel.'

'Agreed. We'll need to see if Frank knows. I'm due to meet him in town in less than an hour.'

'Where?'

'Terrace at the Grand for one-thirty and then after Frank I've arranged to meet Annette Redpath at her office.'

'OK good, I'll see you at the Grand.'

EIGHTEEN

FRIDAY

The Grand Jersey would have once been little more than a stone's throw from the harbour wall, overlooking the road into St Helier where horse-drawn carriages would have trotted by. Nowadays, the road had been widened and the landscape in front of it and to the left, changed by the reclaiming of land from the sea. The Grand still stood looking out over the beach, separated by the road, and stayed true to its name as a five-star hotel. Winter easily spotted Frank sitting under one of the umbrellas on the terrace; he'd obviously had lunch and his guest departed because there were empty coffee cups on the table accompanied by used serviettes. When Winter approached, Frank motioned to one of the waiters to clear the table.

'Mr Mason,' Winter said, holding out his hand. 'DI Winter Labey.'

'We've met before,' Frank said, barely making much effort to lean over and accept his shake. 'One of those fundraisers for victims of violence.' He came across as relaxed rather than rude and was known for never forgetting a face.

'Of course,' Winter agreed. 'I wasn't sure you'd remember. Thank you for fitting me into your schedule, we need to speak to everyone who was at Paul Cabot's house the night of the election.'

'Absolutely, I understand. Nasty business,' he added.

Winter was about to launch into his questions when Frank was distracted by somebody or something behind his shoulder. It turned out to be Saskia Monet approaching. He introduced them, and noted that Frank sat up and firmly grasped Saskia's hand, keeping eye contact. Winter also noted that it had irritated him, dare he say even made him feel a little possessively jealous. He'd need to keep that in check.

'Miss Monet is building up a profile of the killer for us,' Winter explained, attempting to get Frank to look at him rather than Saskia.

'And what do you have so far, Miss Monet?' Frank asked.

'I'm afraid that I'm not at liberty to reveal that, Mr Mason. It's part of the information being gathered during the investigation and you appreciate, of course, that it could compromise the enquiries.' She'd said it pleasantly, but her manner was firm.

Winter began his questions. 'Could you please tell me how you knew Paul Cabot?'

'Paul! Known him for years really, you know how it is. Our circles have merged every now and then. I live in St Brelade and thought he'd make a good candidate, so I said I was happy to endorse his candidature.'

'Did that include paying for social media support for him?' Winter asked directly.

Frank gave him a penetrating stare. 'I have Alfie Chen on a retainer. I offered to loan him to Paul during the campaign to support him, that's all.'

'Was that going to be declared on Paul's election expenses, Mr Mason?'

'I'm sure if we needed to then it would have been.' Frank's reply was final. Winter knew that he could never prove whether they had any intention of reporting it. It also wasn't really his concern right now; what was his concern was why he'd paid for social media support, and could it have anything to do with Paul's murder.

'Why did you lend your support to Mr Cabot?'

'I've told you. I live in the parish and thought he'd be good for us.'

'So it had nothing to do with the fact you were talking to him about buying his property and land and developing it?'

Frank sucked in a lungful of air and let out a big sigh. 'Ah OK, I see where this is leading.' He turned to Saskia. 'Detective Inspector Labey here thinks that I killed Paul Cabot because I couldn't get my hands on his land. That's what you're asking, isn't it?' He looked at Winter challengingly.

'That wasn't what I was asking, but did you?'

Frank laughed. 'No. Do you really think I kill everyone who lets me down in a business deal? You'd be a lot busier if that was the case, DI Labey.'

The conversation was interrupted by the waiter coming to the table and asking if they wanted anything.

'Just a glass of tap water please,' Winter replied, and Saskia also requested the same.

'Are you sure you wouldn't like a bite to eat? It is lunchtime,' Frank asked Saskia.

'No, honestly, I'm fine, thank you,' she replied. Winter wondered if she was just as averse to accepting anything from Frank Mason as he was. Tap water was free.

'So Paul called the deal off?' Winter pushed.

'Yes. On election night. His son had found out about the deal and was upset.'

'Do you know how Daniel Cabot found out about your proposed deal with his father?' Saskia spoke now.

'No doubt it was Matthew Cabot. No idea how he knew, but this island is a nightmare for privacy and gossip. Matthew confronted me about it when I first arrived. He was pretty annoyed, was raging on about how he'd never got anything because it was all supposed to stay in the family and should be going to Daniel.'

'Did Daniel speak to you too?'

'No, just Paul. Said his son had found out and was really upset with him, that it was a stupid idea and he was sorry but he shouldn't have even entertained it and he wasn't going to sell.'

'What time in the evening was this?' Winter asked.

'I left straight after, so it was after one-thirty... maybe one forty-five? Sure, it pissed me off, but not enough to kill the man.'

'Had Paul spoken to Matthew about it too?'

'I don't know. Not that he told me.'

Winter nodded and thought a moment.

'When you left had Matthew and Daniel gone by then?'

'Yeah, Matthew had left an hour or so before with his wife, and Daniel just disappeared up to bed I presume. It was just Tom, George, Joshua, and Paul. We'd been drinking some of the family port. Really nice stuff.'

'Where did you go next?'

'I went straight home. I had a driver on standby so I walked down the road and he met me. I was in bed asleep within twenty minutes of getting in.'

'Can anyone verify that you were home?'

'The driver obviously, and my wife who was none too pleased when I woke her up.'

Winter nodded. 'Thank you, and is there anyone that you can think of who would have reason to kill Paul?'

'No. I mean he was hardly an extremist, was he? He was a pretty anodyne person really, typical of somebody who had never had to work hard to achieve something for himself and just lived in the same house and parish all his life. I think the election win was really important to him. Something he could say he'd done without any help from his father or grandfather.'

Winter and Saskia's glasses of water arrived and they both took the opportunity to take a long drink.

'Apparently Paul was a bit of a little shit when he was younger, according to his mate George. George was pretty plastered and was telling me how Paul used to bully him at boarding school. Sounded pretty nasty. No idea how or why they became friends again, but there you go. Nowt so queer as folk, so my grandmother used to say.' Frank smiled at them both. 'Obviously I'm not suggesting they were queer in the modern sense,' he quickly qualified. 'It's just an old saying.'

Winter thought it was not only a very true saying, but what Frank had just told them was a motive for George Sanchez. The other consideration was Matthew Cabot who might have learnt to live with not inheriting anything, but might have found the news that his brother was thinking of selling up, just a step too far.

NINETEEN

FRIDAY

Winter received a phone call just as they were leaving the Grand.

'I need to take this,' he said to Saskia, and pulled over into a bus lay-by.

They were on their way to interview Annette Redpath.

'OK, mmhm, right...' Winter's responses weren't giving anything away. 'Thanks.' He ended the call.

Saskia sat waiting expectantly.

'So, blood traces in the sink were Paul's, the German antique gun was the murder weapon, but no blood or gunshot residue found on any of the clothing that we seized. That means we have no evidence to say that Joshua, Tom, Daniel, or Vicky, are our killer.'

'But they could have changed,' Saskia said. 'It does at least indicate that the killer was someone who Paul knew and had been in the house.'

'Yes, although Tom and Joshua were in the same clothes as they wore the night before because they slept over. Still, they could have changed into something else if they knew what they were going to do.'

'Maybe, but wouldn't Paul have noticed and found that strange?'

'You'd have thought so, which puts Tom and Joshua as outliers. But we have others in the frame.'

'Yes, we definitely can't rule out Matthew or Daniel – the killing was personal and they certainly knew him well. It sounds like the anger over not inheriting a scrap had lingered for Matthew. Not surprising really. Perhaps he couldn't take the fact that Paul was planning on selling up? Daniel of course is also the main beneficiary. If his father hadn't died he may have lost out on a lot. He didn't know that his father had agreed not to sell.'

'Plus we have the affair. That could implicate Vicky,' Winter added.

'Or Annette Redpath, as well as her husband. Could Paul have called the affair off too?'

'Well, we can ask her that as we're due at her office in ten minutes.'

'I also think you have to seriously consider George Sanchez. Just because the bullying was a long time ago, it doesn't mean that it wasn't a motive. When children are bullied they can get a form of PTSD. He could have buried what for him was a traumatic time and it's only now that it has resurfaced and he acted on it.'

'Really, after all this time?'

'Oh yes, definitely. Something could have triggered it.'

Winter nodded thoughtfully. 'You spoke to Daniel, what do you think about him?'

'I didn't see anything that would indicate he was the murderer. That was a cold-blooded killing, so to do that to your own father would require a very particular type of personality which I didn't see any evidence of... but teenagers are notoriously good liars. They're very self-centred too and prone to emotional decision-making, so perhaps he thought he was justified.'

'Or perhaps someone else was acting on his behalf? Matthew was very defensive of the grandfather who insisted on the farm remaining in family hands after he'd built it up. I'd like to talk to him again. Let's go and see what Annette has to say about the affair. She might have a good idea what kind of mindset Paul was in.'

Annette Redpath met them in a characterless meeting room that the receptionist showed them into. Her face was concrete firm. Saskia could sense she was only just holding it together.

'Thank you for finding the time to talk to us,' Winter started in his usual respectful and polite way. Saskia had noticed he was like this with everyone, even those who she knew annoyed him. She wondered what he'd be like when he was interviewing a firm suspect. Did he ever play the tough cop role? He definitely had it in him.

'Mrs Redpath, as you know, we are investigating the death of Paul Cabot.'

Saskia saw the concrete facade quiver as though an earth tremor had passed underneath.

'I wanted to ask you about your relationship with the deceased—'

'You obviously know that we were having an affair.'

The reply was like a snake biting, fast and deadly. Winter stopped talking and just waited. Saskia approved of the tactic – silence was a fantastic prompter.

The earth tremor came again. 'It wasn't something either of us intended, but my marriage has been going nowhere for a while. I think Joshua and I only stay together because of the children.'

'Was it serious? The relationship with Paul?'

'No. It had only been about six weeks. I regret it totally of course.'

'When did Joshua find out?'

'Day of the election. He'd had to borrow my phone because the battery ran out on his. Bloody stupid. I just didn't think.' She shook her head at herself and looked down as though the error of her ways could somehow be seen in her lap.

'How did he react?'

Annette looked back up at Winter. 'Oh my god, you think Joshua killed Paul, don't you? He wouldn't. That's just not who he is. He was angry, disappointed in me, yes, but...' She stopped talking.

'But what, Mrs Redpath?'

'He told me he didn't. He wouldn't.'

But Saskia could see that Annette was no longer a hundred per cent convinced. There were hairline cracks in her concrete exterior as she contemplated her entire world falling apart.

Winter clearly knew the value in letting something brew and he allowed Annette to contemplate the situation for a few more moments.

'Our investigations are still ongoing. What time did you leave the election party?' he asked her.

'About half eleven, it's a school night and our babysitter is in the sixth form. We couldn't make her stay up any later and, to be honest, I'd rather not have gone at all. Joshua was being so cold towards me, and when I told Paul that he knew, he'd said that we shouldn't ever have started it and it was over anyway. He didn't want to risk anything getting out publicly. Six weeks and a ruined marriage, for what!' Annette's face took on the mask of a victim.

Saskia wondered if Annette had ever stopped to consider Vicky and how she was feeling, as well as her own husband. Could her bitterness that Paul was ending the affair be enough for her to want to kill him?

'How did that conversation make you feel?' Saskia asked her.

Annette focused on her, clearly weighing up the question. 'Angry at Paul of course, isn't that what you're expecting me to say? But not so angry that I'd kill him. He was always preaching the importance of family and yet he instigated our affair, and did you know he was also thinking about selling the family farm to a developer?'

'Did he tell you that?'

'No. Joshua told me. He'd overheard a few conversations between Paul and the developer.'

'Did you tell anyone else about that?'

She shook her head.

'Do you know if Joshua told anyone else?'

'No idea.'

'Do you have any idea why the painting of Paul's grandfather in his study might have been damaged?' Winter asked.

Annette shrugged. 'No. He used to talk about his grandfather sometimes. Had him on a pedestal. It certainly wouldn't have been Paul that did that, he'd have been devastated if the painting was damaged.'

'Did Paul ever talk to you about his son and brother? Was everything fine between them all?'

'I think so, as far as I know. Although from what I've heard they didn't have any idea about the development plans – that would definitely have upset them both.'

Winter looked to Saskia to see if she had any other questions. She didn't.

'There are some items which have gone missing from Paul's house. Two silver inkwells, some first edition books and a couple of glass vases, so we're also investigating a robbery motive to the murder,' Winter said to Annette.

Saskia knew he wasn't telling her that to update her on the police inquiry, it was to see if she might have seen them because her husband had taken them. There was no flicker on her face, no change in her body language, but then perhaps he had taken them straight to the shop – if he'd taken them at all.

Winter was silent as they left Annette's office and returned to the streets of St Helier. There was the smell of rain and a swell of damp in the air. He looked like he had already found himself under a rain cloud; his face was moody.

'What are you thinking?' Saskia asked.

'I'm thinking that Paul Cabot was surrounded by friends and family who all had motives for killing him. Every one of them that we've interviewed could have taken their grudge to the next level, and we haven't finished yet. We've got Tom and George to talk to.'

'So you're definitely discounting a political motive?'

Winter nodded his head. 'Yes. I'm listening to what you said and what's in front of me. I think you're right, this is far more personal and he knew his killer. The question is, which one of them was it?'

TWENTY

FRIDAY

Saskia's first impression of George Sanchez was that he was a man who was lost, stuck in a past world. His house was behind a large wall, the wrought-iron gates wedged open, through lack of usability rather than choice; and so they were able to drive straight in to find themselves in an expansive overgrown garden. The gravel driveway was littered in fallen tree debris, leaves, small branches, and the squashed brown shards of acorns and other tree fruit that was unrecognisable. All the shrubs had been allowed free rein and long, thick branches of buddleia and fuchsias hung over the drive. As they drove past, the little purple and pink ballerina-like flowers of the fuchsias danced around them.

'There's a house in here somewhere,' Winter said sarcastically. In front was a row of palm trees, interspersed with the huge blooms of the *Echium Pininana*, a conical spike of a flower head that was taller than most people and smothered in tiny flowers that were a mecca for bees. Saskia had never seen anything like them until she'd come to Jersey and found one growing in her back garden. June had told her they can pop up like weeds in the island. Saskia found them magnificent.

The house appeared behind all the foliage, a large Victorian property, the kind that would have had a ballroom and servant accommodation. Its walls were once white but were now scarred brown by ivy tendrils, and stained by the weather and mildew, as though they'd been put in the wash with something coloured. 'This place would be worth millions if it was done up,' Winter said to her. 'I wonder what the story is here.'

She thought that for all the bright colours of the flowers, it was a sad and mournful place, as though life for the occupants had stood still while nature carried on regardless. An abandoned graveyard of a once-wealthy family.

As they drew to a halt, the large front door was opened. Somebody had made an amateur attempt to paint it, probably to keep it from rotting, which gave it an almost child-like look. It was larger than an average door, wide enough for a big skirted dress to pass through without touching. Saskia could already see that the hallway looked magnificent. Black and white parquet tiles and a big staircase. It was like stepping into a movie set at the start of a horror film before the action began. All sunshine, cobwebs, and faded grandeur, with an abandoned garden and a reclusive owner.

George Sanchez stood on the threshold of his home looking as pale and mournful as the house.

'Mr Sanchez.' Winter stepped forward and introduced them.

'Come in, come in. You'll have to excuse the mess. I'm not one for housework I'm afraid.' George walked ahead of them, his feet in soft slippers, slopping across the tiled floor, and a moth-hole revealing itself on the back of the cardigan he was wearing. There were big paintings of old-fashioned-looking people around the hall and up the stairs, with pride of place given to a pair of more modern portraits. One was a severe, dark-haired man, who looked distinguished but cold, and the other was of a beautiful young woman. Even from the painted image you could see that she was haunted and in pain. The artist had captured her perfectly: her fragility, her almost other worldliness that drew you towards her in the same way the painting of the man pushed you away. Both Saskia and Winter looked up into her eyes.

'My mother,' George said to them.

'She's very beautiful,' Winter replied.

'She was.'

The doors that accessed the hallway were all closed and George led them under the stairs and to a large kitchen. It was clear that this was where he spent his time. There was a small area where a sofa and chair were positioned in front of a television, and on the other side, a little desk with a laptop.

'I'd been living and working in England since leaving school. My father lived here on his own until his death. You probably know this already but I spent some time in a hospital receiving treatment for my mental health before I came back here.'

Saskia felt for the man. Like many people she'd met, he defined himself by his mental illness. Immediately putting it out there. No doubt spent his time apologising for it as though it was an unwelcome guest in the midst of a conversation. She saw Winter's eyes go to her and knew that he thought she might be better experienced to handle the questioning.

Nevertheless, he began. 'As I said on the phone, we're talking to everyone who was at the Cabot household on election night as part of our investigation into Paul's death.'

George nodded. As he tipped his head down it accentuated the dark-grey circles under his eyes.

Saskia felt Winter's gaze on her again.

'You and Paul were at school together, I understand?' she said to George. Whatever haunted this man was deeply rooted.

'Yes. I was sent to boarding school after my mother died.'

'That must have been hard,' Saskia said to him gently. The pain was more than evident to see even after all these years.

'Yes. Finding your mother dead at eight years old and then being sent to a strange place without friends or family was not my father's most caring move. I don't think he could help himself though. He wasn't a particularly warm person at the best of times, but he was beside himself about my mother's loss, incapable of self-care, let alone an eight year old. It's taken me a long time to forgive him and to get over the feeling of abandonment.'

Saskia wasn't sure he had got over the abandonment issue. George's experience in a mental health hospital was also clear to her. He was used to sitting and sharing. It was therapy. The illness was his shame, but the cause, he'd learnt, wasn't his fault. 'So you met Paul at school?' She nudged.

'Yeah. He'd already been there a year.'

'Did you form a friendship straight away? Two boys from Jersey?'

'Friendship? Oh no. He was horrible to me. I cried every night and every morning he would torment me about my bed-wetting and my tears. He was probably as insecure as I was in this boarding-school world, and it was his way of feeling like he had some superiority. Made him feel better. School was Hell for me. Home life was Hell. I'm afraid my childhood was not the stuff of Enid Blyton books.'

'I'm sorry. That must have been very hard.'

George lifted his eyes and looked at her. 'It was. I left as soon as I could.'

'What did you do after school?'

'I had money. My father gave me an allowance, his way of appeasing his own conscience I guess. That didn't do me any favours either. I travelled for a while, trying to find myself. It took my mental breakdown to make me realise that I'm not totally defined by my childhood experiences, that I have a choice.'

Saskia felt it sounded like he was still trying to convince himself of that fact.

'Did you see Paul during that time?'

George shook his head. 'He'd come back to Jersey. I didn't even return for my father's funeral, I was in the hospital by then. It was only two years ago, once I'd been discharged, that I decided to face up to my past. This place had been empty for a couple of years but it was as though time had stood still since my childhood. Nothing seemed to have changed except my parents were ghosts around the place. But you know what Jersey's like. People gossip, and word got back to Paul that I'd come back and one day he turned up on my doorstep.'

Saskia saw that Winter was about to comment, but her silence encouraged him to also just listen.

George continued, 'Can't say I was overly welcoming, but he had come to apologise. Said that he'd always felt guilty about the way he'd treated me and since he'd grown up and had a son of his own, he'd realised how cruel he had been and what an awful time I must have been having. He stayed for hours. It was emotionally exhausting re-living it all, but I respected him for coming. After that we became friends.'

'You forgave him?' Winter couldn't help himself.

'Yes.' George studied Winter's face. 'Bitterness and anger at someone or something is just destructive for yourself, not them. When we talked I realised just how much poison I'd kept inside of me and it was only myself I was hurting. He was just an eight-year-old kid, same as I was. He'd also been sent away from his home the year before me, had to say goodbye to everything he'd ever known and survive in that new world. He was struggling too. I'm not saying that what he did was OK, because it wasn't. But you shouldn't hang on to that poison. You have to move on, or else it just destroys you.'

George paused and neither Saskia or Winter disturbed the expectant air around him. 'If you think that I could have killed him because of the fact he bullied me decades ago then you're wasting your time. We had made our peace. I'm sorry that he's gone. I enjoyed our long talks together.'

Saskia could see the real sadness in George's face. They'd need to look at the nature of his mental illness, but from how he had presented so far, she didn't see him as a murderer, he presented as more of a danger to himself than someone else. His pain was inward-focused, and yet...

'Frank Mason said you'd talked about the bullying on the night of the election.'

'Did I?' George sighed. 'I shouldn't drink you know, it never does me any favours and I take medication. He probably asked me how I knew Paul.'

When George looked at her this time, his eyes were more defiant.

'You say you had long talks, did Paul talk to you about anything that was worrying him, or anyone he was worried about?' Winter asked.

George thought for a while. 'I'd say he was, as he put it, having a bit of a mid-life reconsideration. Not a crisis, but he'd started to think about his own mortality and wanted to achieve something before he ran out of time. I know that his family and their history were really important to him, but in some ways it was also a cage, a burden of responsibility.'

'Did he tell you he was thinking of selling the farm?'

'He talked about it. Told me I should sell this and enjoy the money. I might well do that. But, if I'm honest, I didn't think he'd go through with his sale. His grandfather and father had been such big influences in his life. It was more like a rebellion plan B – a way to do something of his own if he didn't win the election.'

'Can I ask if you knew why Paul got sent to boarding school

in England? If his parents were so traditionally Jersey, why not educate him here? Send him to Vic?' Winter asked.

George frowned. 'I'm not sure, that's a good point because they were so derogatory about families who had evacuated during the war. I think it was snobbery. They wanted to show they could afford to do it and Paul wasn't really that academic. He struggled a bit at school. Perhaps he wasn't able to get into Victoria College and so boarding school was his only option in their eyes?'

'So there wasn't anyone he was worried about? Anyone he suggested might harm him?'

'No. In the last few weeks, he was the happiest I'd seen him. The feedback he was getting in his campaigning was really positive – he thought he was going to win. It was something he'd achieved for himself.'

'The night of the party, did you notice anybody acting strangely? Any arguments?'

'I think Daniel and Matthew were annoyed about something. Matthew hid it better than his nephew. Paul disappeared off for about half an hour at one point and then when he came back he asked to speak to Frank Mason. I guessed that it might be to do with the selling of the farm as Frank had been the one who wanted it. Nothing much else. Tom was there. They'd been school friends in prep but Tom had stayed on island when Paul went to boarding school so I hadn't known him. The campaign manager was a bit of a cold fish, but I enjoyed chatting to young Alfie Chen.'

'What time did you leave?'

'After the results were called and we'd celebrated with some champagne and port. As I've said, I'm still on medication, shouldn't really drink. It makes me tired as it is. Paul called me a cab. I don't drive anymore.' George saw Winter's questioning eyebrow. 'I lost my licence when I was in England, just before my breakdown. Drinking and driving. Could have killed someone.'

Saskia couldn't help but feel for the man who'd spent the bulk of his lifetime trying to come to terms with his childhood. 'I hope you are able to make that fresh start,' she said to George as they left, but she wondered if he'd ever get out from under the painted gaze of his parents.

Winter was quiet in the car. 'That place was depressing,' he eventually said. 'No wonder he's not getting any better. He needs to get out of that house.'

'I think you're right,' she replied, although she didn't think that it was the bricks and mortar around him that held George Sanchez trapped. His prison was inside his head and wherever he went, he would never find freedom.

'He has a motive but I'm not getting a killer vibe from him, not unless he has a multiple personality disorder. I'll put in some checks and find out the exact nature of his mental illness, just in case. And we'll check with the cab company to make sure he went home. If he doesn't drive then I don't see how he could have gone back to kill Paul.'

Saskia agreed with him about that too. George came across as an underdog, lacking in the confidence to commit the kind of murder that she'd seen at the bunker on Noirmont point. Paul's killer had been determined, confident in their actions. The killer was still out there somewhere.

TWENTY-ONE

FRIDAY

Winter decided to get back to the station and check in on his team and the latest updates. Saskia said she'd tag along too and then head home after the briefing. His head was spinning with the various scenarios in front of them. Even if they could discount George, there were still plenty of others who had potential motives and opportunity to kill Paul.

The team was buzzing with information as they settled into their seats in the briefing room. DCI Sharpe had slunk into the room and was standing at the back, arms folded across his chest. Watching. Winter turned on the screen in front of them.

'OK, everyone, we have a lot to get through. Let's get started. Autopsy report is in. Nothing that we hadn't already expected. Shot to the back of the head at close range. What we do now know is that the murder weapon was the World War Two German pistol that had been replaced in Paul's gun safe. Time of death estimated between two a.m. and five a.m. due to some rigor mortis present. Forensics are still working on his clothing, but even if we do find DNA from the killer, if they're one of the guests at the party then it's not going to help our prosecution case because that could have been transferred during the evening. We do know that the killer definitely returned to the house, washing their hands in the downstairs sink and replacing the hand gun. They also appear to have stolen several items. Anything else from Forensics so far that can help us? What about fingerprints on the gun safe and painting, Andrew?'

'Gun safe had been wiped, we found partials on the picture frame for Paul, Vicky and Tom, but our killer could have worn gloves.'

'We know that Tom and Vicky went into the study in the morning and moved the broken picture frame so that discounts them. So, could Paul have damaged the painting himself? Perhaps he found something out about the grandfather, or perhaps him attacking the painting was the reason why he was then killed...' Winter looked at the room. 'If this was a spur of the moment crime of passion attack, why didn't the killer use the same sharp knife on Paul that they'd used on the painting? Why make that trip to the bunker and use that particular gun? Any luck with CCTV?'

'We have one camera at a property further up the road that recorded cars coming and going and backs up the statements by Annette Redpath, Frank Mason, Alfie Chen, and George Sanchez about their movements. No other cars were seen coming or going until the morning when Joshua Redpath left. That doesn't of course mean that somebody didn't approach from across the fields on foot. There are several routes that go across country and lead to the farmhouse as we know that's undoubtedly how Paul and his killer left. We've not found any CCTV to cover them.'

'So we can't rule out that one of those who left in a car didn't come back on foot, and we still have several potential suspects left at the house including Joshua Redpath.' Winter brought up a photograph of Joshua on the screen. 'He found out that morning that his wife had been having an affair with the man for whom he'd been giving up his own free time to help get elected. Double betrayal, a clear motive for a crime of passion. Add to that the fact he's an antiques dealer. The items which were stolen were carefully targeted, they were the most valuable which indicates that whoever took them knew that. The clothes that he was wearing haven't shown any blood spatters, but could he have borrowed something else to wear from Paul's wardrobe? I want someone to look at how easy it would have been for him to find something else to wear when committing the murder. Perhaps some farm overalls. Have we checked all bins in the area?'

'I can do that, sir,' DC Peter Edwards spoke up.

'Thanks, Pete. Right, next up is Paul's son, Daniel. He discovered that his father was planning on selling his inheritance, his birthright, to Frank Mason. Several people say they argued on election night. Daniel went to bed before Paul spoke to Frank and called off the deal. Did Daniel come back down again later, having brooded in his room, and kill his father? He'd have been easily able to change his clothing and then dispose of it.

'Likewise the brother, Matthew Cabot. He didn't get anything from their father – the whole lot went to Paul. That must rankle. When he heard that Paul was going to sell it all, potentially meaning he would have lost the use of the other farmhouse, and the whole purpose of the inheritance scheme was ruined, did he get his revenge? Easy for him to have come back across the field in different clothes. Matthew was passionate about his defence of their grandfather too, so that could explain the painting damage. Perhaps he and Paul argued and Paul pulled the painting off the wall. That may have been the last straw for his brother.

'Can someone do some more digging into both Daniel and

Matthew Cabot? Any other incidences where they've lost their tempers? What were relations really like between them and Paul? Sarah, you've spent a bit of time with the family, can you do that?'

'Sure, boss.'

'Frank Mason. He had been paying Alfie Chen to run Paul's social media during the election campaign, probably outside of election expenses, and because he thought he was going to get his hands on Paul's properties and land. He told us that on election night Paul called the deal off after Daniel found out from Matthew. We don't yet know who told Matthew, but I wouldn't be surprised if it was Joshua because he'd told his wife that he'd overheard some of the negotiations. I'm dubious that Frank is our killer. The man must be used to setbacks like that, and he said he went home and to bed. Not top of our list, but we need to keep him on the sidelines.'

'Then George Sanchez and Tom Le Feuvre. Paul bullied George as a child, but they'd reconciled in recent years. Did George still hold a grudge? He has had treatment for a mental illness, can somebody check the nature of that please and if it involved violence? The other friend, Tom Le Feuvre, spent the night at the house. He's been friends with Paul since childhood and by all accounts there were no issues in their relationship. We've tested his clothes, no signs of any blood or gunpowder. I can't see any reason why Tom would want to kill his friend, but can somebody dig around and ensure that things were all OK between the pair? Are we missing anything with him?'

'I can do that, sir,' DS Mark Le Scelleur spoke up.

Winter nodded his thanks. 'And, finally, the two wives. Vicky found out about the affair that night, said it wasn't the first time but she went to bed upset. Was this the final straw for her? Then Annette Redpath told us that Paul said their affair was over that night. Was she angry at him for having ruined her own marriage? Or perhaps she was obsessed? She strikes me as the kind of woman who holds it all in, maybe it burst out of her that night.'

Winter turned and looked at the room. All eyes were on him. 'Anything to add?'

Predictably, DCI Christopher Sharpe spoke first. 'What about the political motive? None of these take into account the fact it was election night and he'd just been elected. The mode of death was like an execution. This screams some kind of political killing with a wartime German pistol at a Nazi bunker.'

'That's a valid point, sir. I spoke to Derek Page, he is definitely out of the picture, and Mark caught up with Mary Roberts and Philip Jones who were also trolling Paul during the campaign. All have alibis. You're right that we could have a killer who is totally unknown to us, someone who doesn't agree with Paul's stance, but we've found nothing to suggest his electioneering upset anyone. He wasn't an extremist in any shape or form. I just don't see who would object to him as a deputy enough to kill him.

'Even more critical is the evidence. We know the killer was in Paul's home when there were several other people there. That would be audacious to say the least if you were a stranger – this makes it far more likely that it was someone he knew. Someone who people would expect to see in the house. Someone who also knew that he kept an antique pistol in the safe and knew how to get it open.'

The DCI looked at Saskia. 'Miss Monet, you've had experience in the wider world, do you have anything you want to add about who our killer might be?'

Saskia had been taking everything in, but she could see from the look that the DCI was giving her, that he was hoping she'd back him up. 'I think that from the way he was killed, he knew who shot him. The fact he walked across the fields to the headland with that person also backs that up. This supports the theory that it's one of the family or friends that have just been mentioned and not a stranger.

'I agree that there is also a very strong reference to the war and to past generations in what happened. I don't necessarily think that's political, I think it indicates a deep-rooted grudge. It's not something that materialised just on election night, I think this goes much further back and perhaps the trigger was on election night. This is also backed up by the fact that it wasn't a crime of passion; the killer didn't just grab a weapon in the heat of an argument, they marched across fields, stood over the man and then shot him. That's pre-meditated. For someone who hasn't got a history of violence, that needs a very strong conviction to go through with it. Of course, the bunker and pistol could just be symbolic, but there is no getting away from the fact the killer was acting on deep-seated personal reasons.'

'But the killer could be a member of the community, someone that Paul has known for a long time, but not necessarily from his close family and friends—'

'We've no evidence of anyone else being at the property,' Winter butted in. 'But rest assured we are keeping an open mind, sir. At present I'm following the evidence.'

'Could the killer be female?' DC Edwards asked the question and looked at Saskia.

'It's within the realms of possibility. Women tend not to commit violent murders, as we know, but the style of the execution suggests that the killer thought they were acting to somehow redress a past injustice, or perhaps a current one.'

'Which still leaves us with Matthew, Vicki, Joshua, Annette, or Daniel as the most likely suspects,' Winter interjected. 'The affair between Paul and Annette, and the selling of the land that the grandfather had wanted kept together. Vicki, Annette, or Joshua's revenge, or Matthew's bitterness and Daniel's loss of what was his birthright?'

'Maybe,' Saskia said. In her head she saw the young man,

Daniel Cabot. Could he really be capable of murdering his father in cold blood?

'Truth is we don't know enough yet about any of these people,' Winter said to them all. 'By lunchtime tomorrow I want detailed backgrounds on every single one of them, including Paul. We need to find that deep-seated grudge. Who would want Paul Cabot dead? I want no stone left unturned.'

TWENTY-TWO

FRIDAY

Saskia avoided DCI Sharpe after the briefing – she could see he was still convinced the case had a political motive. Instead, she slipped out and went home, the various suspects whirling around her mind. She'd met them all, one of them should surely stand out as the killer, but of course she knew that it just wasn't that simple.

Many of the convicted murderers she'd met in her prison work could live next door to you and you would never guess what they were capable of. Some you could sense had short fuses that might result in violence – they were like open books. They were the ones most likely to kill as they stumbled drunk out of a bar. A random young man passing by getting a fist in his face for daring to look at them, then falling back and cracking his head on the pavement. Dead. Just seconds of being in the wrong place at the wrong time. But the others... the high-functioning psychopaths, the narcissists, the partner abusers, those who killed to fulfil some kind of fantasy, and those who lash out in anger or hurt. They live amongst us and you'd never spot them in the crowd.

The tide was out and so heading to the beach for some

surfing wasn't an option. What Saskia needed was to do something relaxing which would allow her mind to wander and
perhaps create a little space for some inspiration.

The front garden was getting smothered by weeds and so
she decided to head out with some gloves and do a little bit of
tidying up. Gardening was good for the mind. It worked
wonders for some of her most anxious prisoners, allowing them
to feel as though they were doing something productive. It was a
slow process too, so it forced your mind to slow down. The
soothing rhythm of planting, watering, and weeding provided
an antidote to depression and stress. The impact of being
outside with nature was in itself scientifically proven to boost
mood and self-esteem, and in the prison environment when
inmates could feel trapped and stressed, it provided a release
that studies had even shown could reduce their likelihood of
reoffending.

The threat of rain that had been in the air earlier in the day
hadn't amounted to anything. It happened like that sometimes
in Jersey. Rain clouds would pass by, attracted to France, just
across the water, hugging its warm land mass, and miss their
tiny little nine-by-five island. Like so many islanders, Saskia had
already started to track the weather closely. In London it hadn't
really mattered what the weather was – not unless it was snow
which was very rare and invariably brought life to a standstill.
In the city, you were several layers away from the weather and
environment. Sure, you could get wet walking to work or going
shopping, but you were insulated from experiencing its raw
power.

Here in Jersey, she could look out the window one minute
and see bright sunshine, then half an hour later the sky could be
black and it was heavy rain. Weather systems blew in fast and
also just as quickly blew away again. She felt a part of it, within
it. All around her were big open skies and sea. The weather
radar had become her friend. She could see the clouds

approaching, know when they would arrive and when they would leave. Before she went out in the garden, she'd checked and seen a big bank of clouds heading their way but moving slowly. She'd have about an hour before they hit.

Saskia had changed into a pair of old jeans and grabbed some of the thin rubber gloves she used around the house to protect her hands. She didn't possess any gardening gloves but wasn't expecting to come across anything prickly so the thin rubber would do for now against the green staining and mud.

Her little cottage was one of two on the narrow lane before fields separated them from other neighbours. Further along was a farm complex that had been converted into nice modern properties, but most of the occupants accessed their houses from the other end of the lane so it was generally quiet at Saskia's end. June and her dog Pushki lived next door, but this afternoon June was inside and Saskia could hear Radio 4 playing. Pushki wandered out to see what Saskia was up to, and after a stroke, lay down on June's lawn for a snooze in the sun.

On her knees on the lawn, Saskia could hear the constant buzz of bees and other insects in the flowers around her head. She consciously pushed all of the people and information she'd learnt today from her mind, instead focusing only on what was in front of her. She started to pull the weeds from around the plants: grass, dandelions, and a host of others that she had no idea what they were. There was one tall flowering one, with yellow flowers. She left that for the bees. A patch of yellow dandelion flowers nearly met their end, but were saved by the timely arrival of a bumble bee. Saskia sat back on her haunches and looked at the flower bed. Who decided what was a weed and should die and what wasn't? If the bees liked the flowers then surely they had a purpose?

She sat there for a few moments feeling the warm sun on her shoulders, just breathing in the fresh air, a mix of various flower scents and earth, with a hint of sea salt blowing from the beach which was just a fifteen-minute walk away. She was staring at the plants, but not really seeing them. She was daydreaming, thinking about her life here in Jersey, David, Winter, and what might lay ahead.

She'd never been somebody who had a vision for what her life should be like. Maybe it was because she was just grateful to be out of the traumatic and violent environment of her childhood. When she had made plans they'd had to alter due to one of her family members. Contentment for her was peace and feeling like she was achieving something positive with the prisoners and now with the police. She'd found that here. Work was less stressful, the everyday violence had taken a back step, and David was on an even keel. She could focus on herself for a while.

As she sat on the grass, the air began to change. The humidity rose, the smell of rain returned, and a few minutes later the sun disappeared behind a bank of dark grey clouds. She'd not exactly got a lot done, but it had relaxed her. She was just thinking about going back in when Pushki started barking next door. There'd been no cars so it must be somebody walking past that he'd taken a disliking too. His default mode was friendly rather than protective, so Saskia stood up to see who it was he'd taken against.

Her heart went cold. Standing staring at her from across the lane was Mark Byrne, the psychopathic prison officer from work. His face was impassive. His eyes dead like a shark's. How long had he been there watching her?

Pushki growled and started flinging himself at the wall and gate between his garden and Mark. It seemed like an age to Saskia as she pulled herself together from the shock and reacted, although it was just a few seconds.

'Hi Mark.' She smiled at him. 'What brings you round here? Are you walking the lanes?' She hoped her voice sounded level and calm.

Mark said nothing, he just turned and walked away.

'Pushki, what is all that noise?' June's welcome voice came from next door. 'Saskia, ma luv, what is he creating all that racket for, do you know?'

Saskia sucked in a deep breath and let it go again, trying to ease the tension in her diaphragm. 'A man was walking past.' She turned and smiled at June. 'He's a good guard dog, aren't you, Pushki?' Saskia lent over the wall separating their gardens and stroked the dog who was now panting with all the exertion.

'Well it's a good job you're such a forgiving neighbour,' June replied, picking the dog up and addressing him directly. 'Some people don't like all that yapping and shouting, Pushki. You're lucky that Saskia doesn't mind.'

Just then, the first few drops of rain fell, splashing onto Saskia's face and bare arms.

'Oh my, here comes the rain, we'd better get in,' June said to both her and Pushki. 'He's got an aversion to rain, haven't you?' she said, turning and disappearing back inside her cottage with the dog.

Saskia looked down the lane in the direction that Mark had gone. What had he been doing here? Was it a coincidence, or had he come to intimidate her? Her bet would be on the latter option. She was convinced that he was a psychopath, and it was clear he'd taken against her, right from the first day she'd arrived to work at the prison. But what Mark didn't know was that she'd met far worse than him and survived. He'd met his match if he thought he was going to scare her.

TWENTY-THREE

FRIDAY

After the briefing, DCI Sharpe had motioned to Winter that he wanted a word.

'I've got every elected member in the States of Jersey on my back. They're extremely concerned about the fact that Paul's killer could come for one of them next and that we don't seem to be doing our jobs. We need some progress on this case, DI Labey.'

'I believe we are making progress, sir.' Winter reminded himself to keep his voice calm and not rise to the challenge.

'But you seem to have completely disregarded any link to the political aspect of Paul Cabot's life. That psychologist was talking about the Second World War for god's sake, how could that have anything to do with what happened this week? Most of the people who were around then are either dead or in their dotage. Wake up, man, and look at the circumstances. If you're not able to conduct a proper investigation then I'll have to find someone who will.'

'I am, sir.' Winter looked back at his boss who was staring at him as though he were an idiot. 'I have looked into the political motivations and we've drawn a blank there. I also think it's important to keep an open mind.'

DCI Sharpe shook his head at him like he was a schoolboy who'd just forgotten how to spell *the*.

They could argue all day about it, but it wasn't going to further their investigation.

DCI Sharpe scowled at him. 'I'm not convinced you're being thorough enough. You've got twenty-four hours to come up with some progress. We can't have a prominent member of our community shot in cold blood and be allowing his killer to wander around.'

Sharpe had stomped out of the room and left Winter seething in his wake. There was never any support or constructive criticism from the man, just negativity. He took a few deep breaths to calm himself down and then followed his boss out of the room and headed back to the office.

The team were all heads down researching their respective suspects, or digging in deeper to Paul Cabot's life. Winter sat down and got to work on his decision log, the record they had to keep of why they'd gone down any particular path with the investigation. Some people saw it as a headache, paperwork to cover your back in case somebody made a complaint or something went wrong. Winter liked it as a way of getting his mind in order after he'd been bombarded with information. It made him stop and consider everything again. Were they making the right calls? Had they missed something?

He was mid-way through when Annette Redpath called. She was in tears.

'I found them...' She was sobbing, not the deep sobs of a bereaved person, but the fast, shallow sobs of someone who was panicking.

'What have you found, Mrs Redpath?' Winter asked gently.

'The inkwells, the books and those glass vases. He'd hidden

them in the garage. Oh my god, I don't know what to do. Has he lost his mind? I caused this, didn't I? I made him kill Paul.'

'I'll be over immediately, you stay put,' Winter said to her. The second he was off the phone he called out to DC Sarah Fuller. 'Sarah, I need you now. You too, Jonno. That was Annette Redpath, she's found the items stolen from Paul Cabot's house in her garage.'

'I'll get onto Forensics,' DS Jonathon Vibert replied.

The room had been calm and mellow up until this point, a mature river flowing on a steady course in the inquiry. It had now hit rapids and was bubbling with activity.

'I want Pete and Mark over to Jonathon Redpath's antiques shop, the minute we've confirmed that they are the stolen items, I want you to arrest him.'

It was a ten-minute drive on blue lights to the Redpath home. As he approached, Winter turned the lights and siren off. No need to alert the entire neighbourhood as to what was going on at number four. There was one car in the driveway, in the back was a booster seat. Annette must have picked the children up from nursery and school. That would no doubt be adding to her anxiety.

They didn't need to knock – she had the door open before they'd even got out the car.

Annette walked out of her front door and pressed a button to open the big metal garage door. It swung up revealing a garage that would currently not have room for a car. Boxes were piled up in some areas, bikes, boogie boards, a skateboard, kids' fishing nets and a deflated paddling pool added to the melee of family mess.

'I'd been in here at the weekend searching for the paddling pool so I had a good idea of what was in here. When I got back earlier, I came in to put the pool away and immediately spotted that box over there. It's new. They're in there.'

Annette had pointed to a large white cardboard box which had a champagne brand logo on the side. *No doubt the same brand as they'd all been drinking at Paul's house on election night,* thought Winter.

Jonno put on some nitrile gloves and walked over to look in the box. He carefully opened the lid and reached inside, pulling something out that was wrapped in paper. As he unwrapped it, Winter realised that not only was it the missing inkwell, but that the wrap was one of Paul's campaign posters. Jonno looked over to him and nodded. Winter didn't want to upset Annette any further and so he texted the team at the antique shop. *Stolen goods confirmed. Make arrest of Joshua Redpath.*

'What's going to happen to him? What will you do?' Annette was in front of him, her tear-soaked face a pale blend of fright and confusion.

'We will take your husband in for questioning. Just because he took these items doesn't mean that he also killed Paul.'

'You mean you'll arrest him?' Annette needed extra explanation to get through to her shocked mind.

'Yes.'

'Oh god, he's going to be so mad with me. What have I done?'

'Mummy! Mummy?'

A small child's voice called out from the now-opened front door.

'Coming, sweetheart, go back inside with your sister and watch TV. I'll be in in just a minute.' Annette scrubbed at her face with her sleeve.

Winter knew only too well that eyes that red and puffy didn't go down immediately. The children would know she was upset. And he was about to upset her even more.

'I'm very sorry, Annette, but we are going to have to ask you and the kids to stay somewhere else tonight while we search the house. You aren't obliged to leave, but I would advise that it's going to be more unsettling for the children if you don't.'

'Search for what? What are you looking for?' Panic again, dominating her reaction.

'We have to look to ensure there is no evidence to link your husband with the murder of Paul Cabot.'

Annette Redpath seemed to wobble and Winter put out his hand to steady her elbow, ready in case she passed out.

'This is all my fault. If I hadn't been so weak and vain, so taken in by Paul's compliments and attention, none of this would be happening.'

'We don't know for sure what's happened. You need to focus on taking care of your children. Is there someone you can call to come and pick you up? A family member or a friend?'

'My sister. She'll put us up. It's her daughter who babysits for us. She's going to be so mad at me for having an affair. This is just one big shit show.'

With that final announcement, Annette had walked back into the house leaving Winter to contemplate how often one simple action can so easily snowball into a chain reaction with terrible consequences.

Winter left Jonno and Sarah to oversee the evacuation of Annette and her children, and the briefing of the forensic search team. He needed to get back to the station where hopefully Joshua Redpath would be processed into the custody suite, paired with a lawyer, and ready for questioning. As he drove back, he wondered what kind of reaction they'd get. Would Joshua be contrite and confess? Or was it going to be a series of 'no comment' answers that would leave the inquiry frustrated?

It was late afternoon and as he drove back to the station, his stomach made him aware of its needs. He realised he hadn't eaten since breakfast. As luck would have it, he was driving past one of the M&S Simply Food stores, so quickly swung in to get something to eat. Shopping for food when he was hungry was always a bad move as he tended to buy too much and veer towards the more unhealthy options, like a box of ready to eat honey and mustard mini sausages, and a Meat Feast pizza for later. He also bought a chicken Caesar wrap and a yoghurt with granola that was intended for breakfast, but who was watching! Balancing his purchases in his arms in order to avoid buying a carrier bag, Winter returned to his car and continued his journey back to the station.

As investigating officer on the case, Winter wasn't going to conduct the interview. Pete and Mark had that job and Winter was going to watch on a video link. He settled himself into a seat with his late lunch and prepared to see if Joshua Redpath would give them all the answers they'd been looking for.

The sight that met him on the screen was of a broken man. Joshua Redpath seemed to have folded in on himself overnight. As Winter took his wrap out of the packet, his brain, dominated by the gurgling in his stomach, interpreted the world in food terms. Joshua was a deflated soufflé. The tall man had somehow shrunk, and he looked a decade older than his years. His head hung down, shamed and beaten.

Formalities done, DC Pete Edwards started the interview.

'Could you tell us how items from Paul Cabot's house were found in your garage today? The specific items are—'

'I took them,' Joshua interrupted DC Edwards. 'I took them the morning after the election, as I was leaving. I was angry that I'd volunteered to help Paul Cabot get elected and he repaid me by having an affair with my wife. So I took them as payment for my time.'

'Did you kill Paul Cabot?'

'No. What I did was a stupid, irresponsible, and a foolish thing. I would have taken them back. I was going to take them back, but then Paul was killed and it became impossible. I knew what you'd think, but I did not kill him.'

'You stayed the night at the Cabot household and you have just said you were angry. Was it accidental? Did you not mean to shoot Paul?'

'I'm telling you. I took the items you've found in my garage, but I did not harm Paul. I went to bed and he was alive. I woke up and left without seeing him.' Joshua looked to his lawyer who gave a small nod.

'Could you tell us how you found out about the affair your wife was having with Paul Cabot?' DC Edwards changed his line of questioning.

There was a moment's silence. Winter was expecting another 'no comment'.

'My phone battery was virtually out. We'd been standing welcoming people to the polling station all day. All of us were tired. I asked Annette if I could use her phone and she handed it over. She obviously wasn't thinking. Paul had gone to do something, I can't even remember what it was, but one of the local media had asked if he could be available for an interview after the polls had closed. When I went to text him from Annette's phone, I saw the history. All the texts they'd sent each other arranging their meetings.' Joshua paused a few moments, swallowing down the emotion. Hard.

DC Edwards waited for him to continue, but he didn't.

'That must have made you angry,' the police officer tested.

Joshua looked up at him. 'I gave her the phone back, but I left the messages up so she knew I'd seen them. I wasn't about to air our private business in public.'

'So you didn't talk to Annette about it?'

'We spoke briefly. I made my opinions clear.'

'Did you confront Paul?'

'No. I told Vicky.'

'When was this?'

'After the results. We'd had champagne and toasted the victory, Paul had asked Daniel to go and get the family port from the grandparents' cottage next door. Vicky went to get the glasses from the dining room, I followed her and told her then. Annette had already gone home to relieve our babysitter. I hadn't wanted a scene between the two of them, but I wanted Vicky to know.'

'Then what happened?'

'We drank port. I went to bed.'

'You didn't confront Paul at all?'

'No.' Joshua looked down at his lap.

'You just went to bed and didn't say anything to the man who had been sleeping with your wife?'

Joshua looked up angrily and glared at DC Edwards. 'No. I was overwhelmed with emotion. I didn't feel that I was in the right place to speak to him. I also wanted to talk to my wife properly first. I went to bed. As I said, the next morning, I woke up, still felt bitter about it and so I took a few items. It was stupid. I regret it. But I did not kill Paul.'

'You like antiques, Mr Redpath, is that why you chose to use an antique pistol to shoot Mr Cabot?'

Joshua sighed heavily and shook his head. 'No comment.'

Winter hadn't taken his eyes off the screen, but he'd managed to finish his wrap and was working his way through the box of mini sausages. He knew that the interview was also now effectively over. From now onwards Joshua would say no comment. He'd admitted the theft, he had to, but they had no evidence to put to him that implicated him in Paul's murder. He was there, he had a motive, but that wasn't enough to charge him with the killing.

He watched the broken man on the screen. His world had been shattered. His wife had betrayed him, his reputation was ruined, perhaps even his business. People in Jersey didn't forget. The community was too small for Joshua to hide from the gossip. He knew he shouldn't, but Winter had some empathy for the man. But was he a killer? Who knew what he'd been capable of in the heat of the moment when he'd discovered his wife had been sleeping with the man he'd trusted and supported.

TWENTY-FOUR

FRIDAY

Winter had just returned to the office to check that nothing else had come in relating to the inquiry, when he received a phone call from the pathologist. He saw his name come up on his phone and wondered what it could be – he'd already sent in his report and there had been nothing they weren't expecting. Had he found something new?

'Dr Chaudhry?' Winter answered.

'DI Labey I have something that you will be interested in.'

'I thought the report on Paul Cabot was complete?'

'It is, this isn't relating to Mr Cabot. It's the body that was pulled out of the sea yesterday.'

Winter sat up straight in his chair.

'Mr Allan Hall, I found sea water in his lungs as we'd expect with a drowning, but that wasn't all. It was difficult to spot, a less-experienced pathologist might have missed it,' Dr Chaudhry wasn't a man keen on humility, 'but a sharp object had been inserted into the lower neck of Mr Hall which would have paralysed him, at least partially, but not killed him. He went into the sea alive, but this isn't a suicide.'

Winter was silent for a moment as he took the information

in. 'So you're saying that he was stabbed in the neck before being thrown in the sea?'

'That's exactly what I'm saying. I can see where the knife chipped a vertebrae and the insertion point. It's a bit messy after being in the water a few days, but in the deep tissue, it's clearly there.'

'Could he have done this himself?'

'No. The entry wound was too straight. Even if he had managed to somehow get the right level of force behind the back of his head, he would have been completely unable to then throw himself into the sea. I would find it incredibly unlikely that he did this to himself. I'm not going to tell you how to do your job, DI Labey, but I'd say this looks like a murder staged as a suicide.'

'Thank you, will you be able to get something over to me this afternoon?'

'Well, technically speaking, DI Labey, we are now into the evening. It's gone six and I have a gin and tonic waiting for me in my garden along with a lobster salad, but I'll get an initial couple of paragraphs over to you now so you can set the ball rolling and then a full report tomorrow.'

'Thank you, I appreciate it.'

'Have a good evening,' Dr Chaudhry replied, but didn't wait for any more small talk. Clearly he was worried his G and T was going to get warm.

Could Allan Hall's death be in any way related to Paul Cabot? He didn't think so, but two murders in one week on their small island was unusual. Winter pulled up the file on the case. Standard procedures had been followed, statements taken from those closest to Allan; Jackie Slater, his employer, and her partner, David Carter. Plus Allan's partner, Kevin Baker. He'd received a text from Allan saying he was upset and wanted to see him, but when he got round to the house, he said that he wasn't there. Mr Carter had overhead an argument between the two of them on the Friday, the day Allan was last seen. Was Kevin Baker lying? Some studies suggested that domestic violence was higher in same sex relationships than heterosexual ones. Did that argument result in Allan's death?

Winter looked at the time and sighed. Dr Chaudhry was right, any sane person would be clocking off for the day and heading home to enjoy the summer evening. He looked back in Allan's folder and found the phone number of Jackie Slater and dialled it before he regretted it.

'Ms Slater? It's Detective Inspector Winter Labey of States of Jersey police. Would it be convenient for me to come round to have a quick chat and look around Allan Hall's flat?'

Jackie didn't sound overly pleased about the suggestion. 'It's nearly seven o'clock!'

'Yes, but something has arisen in our inquiries and I wanted to talk to you.'

There were a few moments' silence. 'Of course, yes. If you think it's necessary.'

Winter looked at who in his team was still in the office. The only person who was packing up to leave and looked like they'd finished, was DC Potter, but he was loath to ask her to come with him. Amanda had a daughter with Down's syndrome and he knew that it was incredibly difficult for her to always be doing overtime. It must be tough enough juggling the additional needs of her daughter with the job, he wasn't going to ask her to stay longer. Anyone else who was left, was working flat out on the Paul Cabot case, looking into the various suspects' backgrounds. He'd go himself. Get a feel for Jackie Slater and David Carter, and for the kind of person that Allan was. He'd also need to go and see his partner, Kevin, but that might have to wait, depending on what he found tonight. Then he'd need to make a decision on whether this was or wasn't related to Paul's death, and take his findings to his boss to work out how they were going to investigate it.

. . .

Winter Labey drove through a gated entrance into the grounds of a house that wasn't huge, but was certainly larger than average, and one of the most stylish homes he'd seen. It had clearly been extensively renovated, and was a pretty white and granite house in a French style, with a large garage block and extensive gardens. His car scrunched across the gravel and as he came to a stop, a handsome man with black hair and piercing blue eyes opened the front door.

'DI Labey?' he said, extending his hand, 'I'm David Carter, Jackie's partner. Please come in. Would you like a drink?'

An ice-cold beer danced in front of Winter's eyes for a few moments before he replied, 'I'm fine, thank you.'

'If you're sure? Come on through,' David replied.

He led him into a sitting room that was as Winter would imagine the guest parlours used to be like in the older days. Kept for best, with the finest furniture and ornaments and not a speck of dust allowed.

Inside he found an older woman, who stood up as he came in and smiled in the practised, smooth way that someone used to dealing with people in business could do. Winter judged that Jackie Slater was a good few years older than David, although she'd sought some assistance to retain the facade of youth. They were a good-looking couple. He cynically presumed her money was more of the attraction, but then admonished himself for making a judgement without the facts.

'Jackie Slater,' she said to him as he took her hand.

'Thank you for agreeing to speak to me at such short notice. Some information has come to light in the death of Allan Hall and I wanted to just check a couple of things with you both.'

'Absolutely, please fire away, detective,' Jackie said.

Winter looked at the two of them, both perched on the edge of the sofa opposite him like two eager graduate interviewees.

'Do you know if Allan knew a man called Paul Cabot?'

'Cabot? Isn't he the deputy who's just been murdered?' Jackie asked, surprised.

'Yes. That's correct.'

Jackie pulled a face and seemed to be concentrating. 'I don't think so.'

David shook his head too.

'Has anything been stolen from your home in the last week?' Winter asked now.

Jackie frowned. 'Stolen? I don't think so, but we haven't really looked. What kind of things?'

'Anything that's potentially valuable.'

Jackie looked at David who gave a small shake of his head. 'I can't say we've noticed or looked. I suppose your jewellery would be the most valuable, wouldn't it, darling?' David said to her.

'I'll go check now,' she said, 'but I'm pretty certain it's all there.'

Jackie exited the room and Winter was left alone with the man with the piercing blue eyes.

'I understand you overhead an argument between Allan and his partner?' Winter said to him.

'Yes. I could only hear one side of the conversation unfortunately, but Allan was shouting and seemed upset.'

'And you never saw him again after the Friday?'

'No.'

'What about Kevin Baker, did he visit the property at all?'

'I thought I heard somebody arriving later that Friday evening. It sounded like Kevin's car engine. He went into the flat because I heard the door slam, and later he left. But I'm sorry I didn't see anything. I was in the back garden and then the house.'

'Was there ever any indication that Allan was in a coercive relationship?'

David looked a little surprised at the question.

'I don't think so but it's very difficult to know what goes on behind closed doors.'

'Indeed...' Winter was about to continue, but the sight of a pale-faced Jackie re-entering the room distracted him.

'My birthday necklace has gone.'

'Oh my god, darling, are you sure?' David asked, jumping up.

Jackie nodded, stony-faced. 'It was a necklace I bought myself for my fiftieth birthday, inspector,' she addressed Winter, 'worth around forty-five to fifty thousand pounds.'

'And you're absolutely sure it's gone? It's not just been put somewhere differently?'

'I'm one hundred percent sure. I always put it back and I haven't even worn it for weeks, but I know it was there before I went to England because I was looking for something else to wear over there.'

'Can I ask you please to do a thorough search of the property, just in case it has been misplaced, and to also give me information and a photograph of the necklace and the box it is in?'

Jackie nodded sadly.

'I'm so sorry, sweetheart,' David said to her, taking her hand and rubbing the backs of her fingers with his thumb. 'It's not nice to think that someone has taken something like that. Especially something that means so much.'

'You don't think this has anything to do with Allan, do you?' Jackie asked Winter. 'He would never do that to me.'

'I can't say that it's definitely linked, but we certainly need to consider it. Did Mr Hall have keys to this house?'

Jackie's chin creased and she nodded her head.

'And was the house left unattended at any point on the Friday?'

'I left for London mid-afternoon and David was at work,' Jackie said, looking to her partner to take up the story.

'Yes. I got back usual time, must have been between half five and six,' David replied.

'So the property would have been empty for two or three hours?' Winter confirmed.

The pair of them nodded.

'And were you in all weekend, Mr Carter?'

'Most of it. I may have popped out a couple of times but not for long, just to go to the gym.'

'OK. Please can you let me know once you've had the chance to double-check that the necklace hasn't been misplaced, and send over the photographs. We may need to get Forensics in too just in case we can find any fingerprints.'

'Of course.' Jackie slumped back down onto the sofa.

'Can I also ask you both not to go into Mr Hall's flat again? I'm going to need to get a forensics team in there.'

The two people in front of him nodded.

This was not what Winter needed right now, but at least it might turn out to be a simpler case than the Paul Cabot murder. They were going to need to pay Kevin Baker a visit.

TWENTY-FIVE

FRIDAY

Winter took a look at his emails after he'd got back in his car which was parked in Jackie Slater's drive. There was one from Saskia and his stomach did the by-now-familiar flutter at the sight of her name. He was going to have to get over that. She wasn't interested. She had sent her profile of the killer based on what she'd reviewed and seen. He emailed back saying he'd quite like to chat through it when she had some spare time, and was delighted to get an instant reply back.

Free now if it helps.

It would certainly help on more than one front. He missed their chats on the beach, but tonight was not one of those nights. The rain that had rolled in earlier, had rolled off again, but it had left behind cooler air and a breeze. With the sun about to set, it would get even chillier.

Have you eaten? I haven't, so we could meet and chat over some food? As Winter pressed Send, his stomach clenched. Would she take it the wrong way? Could that simple question change their relationship? If she thought he was trying to hit on her she might back away and they'd been getting on so well. He stared at his phone screen, refreshing the list in his email inbox in the hope of seeing her name reappear, unread.

She replied. *Great idea. Let me know where's easiest for you, or if you want to get a takeaway you're welcome to come to mine if it's going to be quieter/more private.*

Winter hadn't been inside her cottage yet. He'd picked her up from there but he'd not got past the garden. He was intrigued to see what kind of home she had, what clues he could find out about her and where she'd come from. Would she have photographs of her parents, mementos from past holidays and friendships? She was quite cagey when it came to talking about herself and he was curious. He wasn't too far from her house so he typed back, *A takeaway at yours sounds perfect. Friday night will be busy and noisy. I can pick something up en route, what do you fancy? Fish and Chips, Chinese, Indian, pizza?*

Whatever's on your way, all good, she replied.

So, she wasn't a fussy eater – that was another plus point. It was Friday, traditional fish and chip night, and he knew a good takeaway that wasn't far. Winter gave a final look at the house where Jackie Slater and David Carter lived, thinking that tomorrow he'd be needing to launch a second murder investigation. He drove off with the hope that not only would he be finding out more about who Paul Cabot's murderer might be, but he'd also get to know the illusive Saskia Monet a bit better.

Thirty-five minutes later, having texted Saskia that the fish and chip shop queue was longer than expected, and did she want vinegar, Winter pulled up outside her cottage. Their dinner had filled his car with the smell of fried potato and warm vinegar and his stomach had reminded him how long ago it was that he had paid it any attention. He'd left the rest of the food he'd bought at M&S at work. It would have to do for tomorrow's breakfast. He was careful not to put the fish and chips on his car seat, mindful that the grease might soak through onto the upholstery.

As he walked up Saskia's garden path with his warm wrapped packages, his stomach was alternating between hungry gurgles and an excited fluttering. When she opened the door, he was briefly lost for words. She looked amazing, even better than usual. Her long hair looked like it had been brushed with silk and her hazel green eyes pulled him in. She'd given him a big smile and he realised that after forcibly shutting his mouth, it had fixed into a grin. She was going to think he was some kind of idiot.

'Fish and chip delivery, ma luv,' he said to her in the colloquial Jersey way.

'Marvellous, I've got cold beers, sparkling water, or pinot grigio.' She peered at his car behind him. 'Appreciate you're driving though.'

'I'll have a cold beer, thank you,' he said following her into the little cottage.

There was a tiny hallway with a door leading to the left that was the sitting room, and a door to the right that was the kitchen. The stairs were directly in front. Winter took in everything, looking for Saskia's stamp on the place. They walked into the kitchen first and she pulled plates and cutlery out. He looked around; the kitchen was clean, had clear surfaces and was functional. There was no calendar or fridge magnets, no ornaments or clutter on the windowsill, nothing that could give away any personality.

'You can wash your hands here, or there's a downstairs toilet under the stairs. Watch your head though, it's not the tallest ceiling.'

'Thanks,' Winter replied, becoming aware that he didn't seem to be capable of fluent conversation. Maybe the beer would chill him out a bit. His bladder niggled on cue and so he'd gone back into the hall and found the small door under the stairs. She was right about the head room and he over-compensated by dipping his head, keen not to get knocked. The toilet was clean and an oil diffuser meant the air smelt good. It wasn't a synthetic cheap smell like you get in some toilets, but a rich aroma, infused with essential oils. Other than that, there was no other indication of who Saskia was in here either. No photo collage of friends and family like some people put in their toilets, no amusing toilet humour or books to read while on the loo.

'In here,' he heard Saskia call out to him from the sitting room when he'd finished, and walked in to find her sitting at a small table at the far end where windows looked out into a near-dark garden. She'd sat herself down and he joined her, his cold beer and fish and chips waiting. Ketchup and mayonnaise were also on the table, along with some salt and pepper.

'Thanks,' he said as he sat down.

'Thank you for bringing me my dinner.' She beamed back at him. 'How has it gone today? Any developments?'

Winter had just put a particularly crispy piece of batter and fish into his mouth and so nodded at her before passing on the news about Joshua Redpath.

'I can totally get why he's done that in a moment of anger,' she replied thoughtfully, 'it suits his character. He's somewhat introverted, but clearly loves antiques and feels comfortable around them. I think I'd have been raging if I'd just given up weeks of my own time to help somebody and they'd repaid me by having an affair with my wife.'

'Yeah, I don't think anyone would blame him, although he has got to be charged. What he did was illegal. Question is, did he also kill Paul?'

Saskia put a chip on her fork and dipped it into the small pile of ketchup on her plate before eating it. 'He doesn't fit the profile.'

Winter looked at her. He'd not noticed before, but there were a few small freckles on her nose.

'Tell me about the profile,' he said to her, dipping one of his own chips into some ketchup. His plateful was fast disappearing – he'd been even hungrier than he'd realised.

'Like I said earlier, the roots of this go back over the generations. The painting, the bunker, the German handgun, all point to that. If it was just a modern-day gripe, why not use one of the more modern guns which were in the safe next to it? It's more reliable, and why go all the way to the bunkers? I still don't think that was just to get him away from the house. These things are all significant to the killer.'

'Male or female?'

'Could be either. As I said before, the way in which Paul was killed, facing away, in the dark, suggests the killer had a connection and some semblance of regret or second thoughts. It wasn't done in the heat of passion, it was almost military-like, a necessary execution. This person felt like it was something they had to do.'

'Which makes me think of either one of the wives, or Matthew or Daniel. I keep circling back to them. Vicky had been shamed for the umpteenth time, maybe she'd had enough? Matthew was the man who lost out to their grandfather's dictate that only the eldest son should inherit in order to keep all the property in one piece for future generations. It must have been galling to hear that Paul was thinking of selling it all. Likewise Daniel, he was set to inherit it all and his dad was about to sell the whole lot from underneath him.'

'Or perhaps Vicky was protecting her son's inheritance? Mothers can do some extreme things in order to protect their children.'

'Now that's true. She had twice the reason to kill her husband.'

'Annette Redpath was from England, and her personality is

too controlled. If she was going to kill Paul, I can't see her doing it like this,' Saskia said to him.

'So, Vicky, Matthew, or Daniel. Plus Tom Le Feuvre stayed overnight, and George Sanchez could have left and gone back. We've checked out Frank Mason's alibi and it sticks. He has video on his front-door bell which fits with his story. The wife also verified it. I didn't think his motive was strong enough anyway. Alfie Chen went into St Helier and we have him on CCTV, so he's a no.'

'Tom is a childhood friend of Paul, right? He's also Jersey born, but what motive could he have?'

'Nothing we've found so far. His clothes also tested negative for any kind of residue and he slept there overnight in them. I saw him in the morning – he was still there when we went to inform Vicky about Paul being found. But he'd known Paul all his life and apparently their families had been close too.'

'I'd check out the history of their two families. Is there anything that could have come to a head on election night?'

'Can't see it, but I'll get someone to have another dig. George has more of a motive, and he's quite a fragile personality. We know that Paul bullied him as a child.'

'Mmhm. When you say *fragile personality*, what exactly do you mean?'

Winter suddenly felt ill-equipped. He'd forgotten he was talking to a psychologist. 'Well, you know, he'd not had a great childhood at home, nor at school. Discovered his mother's body when he was very young and was then sent away to boarding school.'

'Yes, that can result in personality disorders; he might be unable to process his emotions properly and so that could lead to anti-social behaviour. We see plenty of people like that in prison. If he was harbouring a long-held grudge against Paul from the days when he was bullied, then seeing him achieving success in the election could have triggered something. He's also Jersey born.'

Winter nodded. 'True.'

'So, he's going to understand why the occupation means so much, and perhaps he's used that as some kind of metaphor. The only piece that doesn't fit is the grandfather's picture, but maybe it was unrelated, just like the theft probably was. If I'm honest, I agree with you and don't think he has the confidence to have pulled this off.'

Winter forked his last piece of battered fish. 'Anything else that strikes you?'

'Paul's complete compliance. There was no indication of any kind of struggle. This again defies the political theory that DCI Sharpe was professing, and it also indicates something else. I mean, I don't know for sure because I wasn't there, but the compliance goes beyond just being caught out by surprise by a friend or family member, he seems to have accepted his fate, almost as though he himself agreed with his guilt.'

'Can you explain?'

'Sure, work with me on this,' Saskia said, 'and act this out. It will explain it far better.'

'OK,' Winter replied, popping the last piece of fish into his mouth. He was more than happy to do anything she asked him.

'Come with me and walk across to the other side of the living room.'

Winter took a swig of his beer and stood up. It was only a small room, but once on the other side, Saskia picked up the TV remote and pointed it at him.

'This is a gun. I'm going to shoot you now because you very obviously gave yourself the larger portion of fish and chips.'

'No I didn't,' Winter replied, suddenly indignant. *Did she really believe that?*

'Turn around and kneel,' Saskia said to him, her voice hard and commanding.

'No, I seriously didn't take the bigger portion. Anyway, you put them out,' Winter argued.

'Kneel.' Saskia pushed the end of the remote control at him. 'You're just greedy.'

Winter knelt, but carried on arguing. 'Honestly, I'm telling you, I didn't. I wouldn't.'

'OK, *bang*,' Saskia said. 'Now remember how your body is, how you're positioned. Let's go back over there and do it again.'

Winter got up and followed her. He had to concentrate. He was enjoying being up close to her too much.

'Come with me,' Saskia said again to him, and when they got over to the other side, she picked up the remote again. 'You bought fish and chips,' she added, 'and they're not the healthiest meal to have brought round, are they?'

'Mmhm, no I guess not.'

'Kneel and face the door,' her tone changed again. 'Do you not feel just a little bit guilty about having eaten a full plate of deep-fried food? And enticed me to do the same?'

Winter knelt down and thought about what she was saying. 'I do, but I don't get them very often.'

'But you agree they're not the healthiest food to eat?' she said.

'I guess.'

'*Bang*. Now look at your body position.'

Winter snapped out of the thoughts of deep-fried-food guilt and looked at himself.

'You have slumped down, your shoulders are rounded, your weight is on your lower legs, and you're facing away from me. You've accepted your guilt. Before, your body was rigid, you kept twisting to argue with me. If I'd really shot you, the chances were that you would have slumped to the side, or that I might have not been able to get you in the centre of your head, or even more likely if this had been real, you'd have physically fought back. Paul did none of that. He did exactly what you did when you felt your guilt for buying the fish and chips. He slumped down and accepted it. When the shot came, he just tipped forward slightly, his body weight already centred.'

Saskia had come round to stand in front of Winter, who was still kneeling on the floor.

'We have to look at how the victim behaved as well as the motivations of whoever shot him. Paul knew his killer, and he accepted his guilt.'

Winter looked up at her.

'You can get up now if you like.' She raised her eyebrows cheekily at him. 'But you're also welcome to stay on your knees.'

Winter would have liked to pull her down to him and kiss her right there and then, but instead he got up off the floor. 'I can see what you're saying. Nobody would want to kneel in that place. You'd know you were likely to die, but even if he hadn't believed that, if he'd thought there was a chance he could persuade them not to kill him, he would have resisted kneeling on that floor. His body position did look as though he'd given up, accepted his fate.'

'The only other thought I had was that he was protecting somebody else. That by taking the punishment, he could prevent someone he loved from being hurt. That's another possibility we can't ignore. That it wasn't guilt but simple acceptance of the situation.'

'Either way, political motive is definitely out and we need to look more closely at those six people who were closest to him: Matthew, Daniel, Vicky, Gill, Tom and George.'

Saskia sat on the sofa and Winter followed her lead.

'You don't really think I gave you the smaller portion, do you?' he said to her.

She laughed. 'No. I put them out. I gave you the bigger portion,' she said. 'And for the record, although it's not the healthiest food option in the world, I didn't care about that either, they were delicious. Thank you.'

They stayed looking at each other for a little longer than was professionally acceptable, their eyes locked together. He couldn't help himself. Did she feel like he did? It was just so easy being around her. He forced himself to look away, scanning the space around him for any signs of her past life. There was nothing. Empty picture hooks were on the wall, and the shelving space was devoid of anything but books.

'Enjoying living here?' he asked her now, realising it sounded a bit of a pathetic question, and admonishing himself for the way he was thinking. It was like he was going to buy a puppy and wanted to see the dog's parents to check its temperament and credentials.

'I am,' she replied, her eyes on his.

He could feel the pull between them, like magnets. Neither of them seemed as though they wanted to take their eyes off each other. His heart was beginning to pound, and he just talked to try and fill the decreasing gap between them.

'It's looking like I might have another murder inquiry on my hands,' Winter said, not knowing what else to say.

'Another one?' Saskia said in surprise.

'Yes. A chap called Allan Hall was found off St Catherine's. He'd been missing a few days. Jackie Slater the developer had reported it because he worked for her. Looked like he'd just drowned, but the pathologist has found a knife wound.'

It was as though a spell had been broken. Saskia snatched a breath and looked away from him.

'That's terrible. I'd better clear our plates up. My cat, Bilbo, will be on the table otherwise,' she said and hurried across to the table.

Did she think he was going to ask her to help with the new case too and wasn't keen? Is that why she'd reacted like this?

'You know if you ever feel like you can't help us with murder inquiries and profiling, you only have to say. I fully

understand that you must be really busy up at the prison as it is,'
he offered.

Saskia paused as she walked past him with the plates. 'I
will. It's fine. Do you want anything else to drink?'

After that, the conversation was polite, professional, and the
chemistry nil. The only thing that Winter could think was that
Saskia didn't want to get involved with him for whatever reason.
That their closeness had become a little too close for her liking.
He'd been so sure she felt the same as him for that first hour.
Perhaps he'd just been kidding himself. She was nice,
hospitable, and answered all his professional questions, but her
eyes avoided his. He was going to have to shelve any ideas he
had about them having anything other than a purely professional relationship. Winter drove home feeling deflated.

TWENTY-SIX
FRIDAY

What had she been thinking? She had yearned to reach out and kiss Winter. They were just two feet away from each other on the sofa. She'd wanted to touch him, feel his arms around her. Hell, she'd even contemplated asking him to stay the night. Then the bombshell. Allan's death had been murder. The man had been killed while Jackie was away and David and Allan were alone. Had David fooled her? Had he learnt to manipulate and lie so well that he'd lulled her into a false sense of security? Had he killed Allan?

She'd had to get out of the room, allow the shock to wash over her and her mind to stop spinning. Winter was a police officer, he was the man who investigated murders. He was the man who might investigate her brother. He was the man who could put her brother in jail and potentially ruin her own reputation. Saskia had changed her name to her mother's maiden name, years ago. She had no connection to her father, the serial-killing psychopath, and no obvious connection to her brother who'd retained their father's surname. But, if David felt threatened, he could tell all, spill the entire dirty bucket of family secrets onto Winter's lap. He certainly wouldn't fancy having a relationship with her then. Worse still, David might just turn on Winter and kill him if he had the chance.

She'd been an idiot for even contemplating getting closer to Winter. It threatened her, David, and him. No matter what she felt, she was going to have to keep a professional distance. Keep them all safe.

Saskia had taken a few deep breaths, returned to the sitting room and played the perfect host, but without any extras. She was going to need to see David as soon as she could. Confront him about Allan.

After Winter had gone, she'd paced up and down her sitting room until gone midnight, her mind running over all the scenarios and how she might help David and herself in the worst-case outcomes. She'd always known that having a relationship was going to be extremely unlikely, especially with a police detective. She would have to settle for just being friends and hope she never had to compromise their relationship and his trust in her in order to help her brother.

But what if David had done it? What if he'd murdered Allan Hall? Could she keep quiet and allow him to continue living in society where he might hurt again? Was she going to have to give up her brother to the man she was falling in love with?

TWENTY-SEVEN

SATURDAY

Despite the disappointment of the previous night, his talk with Saskia had been very useful and her profile was enlightening. It was the weekend, but, in the middle of a murder inquiry, that didn't count. DI Winter Labey was up, showered, and just about to leave for work by eight a.m. He was eager to get back in to see if the team had found any evidence which could link Joshua Redpath to the murder of Paul Cabot. He was ninety-five per cent positive that they wouldn't have, and was looking forward to getting rid of that distraction and focusing on finding the murderer; that was until he got a WhatsApp message on his phone that made his blood pressure rocket. It was from Jonno.

You seen Bailiwick Express *news?*

There was a link which Winter clicked on. Jonno would only WhatsApp him outside of their official comms channels if it was something he wasn't going to like and might vent about.

The headline on the online Jersey news site was, *Arrest made in Murder of elected Deputy.* The article was quoting DCI Christopher Sharpe who said that the inquiry had progressed and an arrest had now been made in connection with the murder of Paul Cabot.

FFS, Winter texted back to Jonno, then walked out of his flat, slamming the front door.

Winter didn't bother talking to the DCI, he went straight above his head to the chief constable. 'Sir, this is Jersey. People know that we've arrested Joshua Redpath, they are now going to think he's suspected of murder and we haven't got an ounce of evidence to prove that fact. We know he stole the antiques, but there's nothing to say he killed Paul.'

The chief constable read the *Bailiwick Express* report and frowned. 'OK, I'll get a press release out to clarify. So are you going to charge Redpath?'

'With theft, yes. But we'll have to let him go today because we've got nothing else and that's not serious enough to keep him in. His brief will claim diminished responsibility anyway. The man had just found out that Paul had been sleeping with his wife, despite all the hours he'd volunteered to help get him elected. I can't see anyone not having some sympathy for him.'

'Unless he went on to kill him as well...' the chief replied.

'Agreed, but like I say, we've nothing. The search of his home hasn't unearthed anything else. We've had officers at the antiques shop, but found nothing. His clothes were blood and gunshot residue clear. We've searched the entire Cabot property for any signs of clothing worn and contaminated.'

'OK. I'll talk to Chris.'

Winter stood outside the chief's office and stared out the large window that looked towards the sea. He could feel the rage in him and he needed to calm that down before he went back into the office, just in case he came face-to-face with Sharpe and said something he might regret. He could do with a session in the gym punching a bag. The tight knots of anger in his muscles were not going to go away without some help.

As he walked in, Jonno stood up and intercepted him.

'Alright?' he whispered.

'Yeah. I'm fine, don't worry, I'm not going to blow up at that excuse of a detective. I spoke to the chief officer and he's going to put out a press statement making it clear that the person we've arrested has not been charged with Paul's murder. I need to go and speak to Vicky though, let her know what's been going on. Any new leads?'

'Not yet. You cutting Redpath loose?'

'Yeah, but we should give it until late morning once the release is out. I don't want him going out into a community that thinks he's a murderer. I also must speak to the family first. Let him loose in two hours. Give his wife, Annette, a call and let her know too. Those two have a lot of talking to do.'

TWENTY-EIGHT

SATURDAY

It had been in the back of his mind since he first heard the news about his brother's death. The bunker, the gun, the painting of their grandfather. History never goes away, it just lies dormant, waiting to be rediscovered and living in the veins of those who have followed. He'd thought about telling the police detective who'd come round the house, about his suspicions. He was from Jersey too. He'd understand it all. But what should he say? What if he was wrong? So he waited. Waited to see if there was another explanation. Why air the family's dirty laundry in public if they didn't need to? It had never crossed his mind that he could be in danger too.

He'd taken the dogs for their morning walk in the fields. They always say you shouldn't have regular habits because anyone who wants to find an opportunity to attack you, will know when to strike. But, of course, they'd know anyway.

They were waiting in the corn field. The heads of the maize weren't quite ripe, but the stalks were tall, tall enough to hide a person until you were right up close. Matthew had tried not to show his shock when they stepped out. If he looked frightened then they'd know he suspected them. Instead he'd tried to act normal. They'd walked a short way, the dogs running on ahead of them, in and out of the maize hunting rabbits, rats, and pheasants.

For a short while there'd been silence. Just two people out enjoying a summer's morning with the dogs, and then they'd started talking. Matthew knew then what their intentions were. He tried to walk towards the road, or back in the direction of the house, but that's when things turned.

'I knew that you would guess,' they'd said to him. 'How many others know?'

'No one else. You can't blame me, I had nothing to do with it.'

'You're still a part of it.'

Matthew had run then. Started running for his life. The closest house was Paul's and so he'd headed towards that, but he hadn't got far.

TWENTY-NINE
SATURDAY

Winter felt moderately better once he'd left the station and was driving out towards St Ouen. Perhaps it was the memory of driving that way to go surfing. He could trick his mind into thinking he was about to have some fun. The effect didn't last long. His mind soon went back to thinking through the case. He wanted another word with Matthew and Gill Cabot while he was there – he was still not convinced it wasn't a family feud. He'd not considered Gill seriously as a suspect, but she could have been equally as annoyed at Paul as her husband. It was her home too that they stood to lose.

He knocked on the door of Vicky Cabot's house, and it was quickly answered. Vicky was pulling on a pair of shoes.

'DI Labey,' she said, surprised.

'Have I just caught you on your way out?'

'Yes. Gill's just called. Matthew took the dogs for a walk about an hour and a half ago. The dogs have arrived back at their house without him and are extremely agitated. I was just going to go out and see if he's fallen or something. It's been a big shock, these last few days.'

Behind Vicky, Daniel came down the stairs, still pulling on a T-shirt. 'What's happening? Is Uncle Matt OK?'

'He's fine.' Vicky turned, attempting to smile reassuringly at her son.

'I thought I heard a gunshot earlier,' he said to them both.

Winter's hackles rose on the back of his neck. 'I'll come with you. Do you know if he took a regular route?'

'He walks through the fields. Means he can check on the crops at the same time,' Vicky answered.

'What's happening? Where is Uncle Matthew?' Daniel asked again.

Vicky sucked in her breath and turned to him. 'I'm sure he's absolutely fine. He's just a bit late back after his morning walk. I'm going to help Gill look for him.'

'I'll come too,' Daniel replied, walking straight to the shoe rack.

'I'm not sure that's—' Vicky started.

'I'm coming,' Daniel replied firmly.

Daniel had already taken on the mantle of 'the man of the house' and as he seemed close to his uncle, Winter could understand why he wanted to help. They didn't have time to argue.

'Has he got a mobile with him?' Winter asked.

'No,' Vicky answered. 'Gill's tried it and it's at home. She's bringing the dogs in the hope they might lead us to him.'

Winter followed Vicky and Daniel out of the door, through the yard and out the gate into the fields. A path ran along the side of the field and in the distance they could see Gill and the two dogs heading out of their yard and joining the same path at the other end. The first field was empty, nothing but dusty brown earth and a selection of green vegetation that had taken advantage of the fact the potatoes had been dug up and were trying to lay claim to the space. In front of them though, were several fields of maize. A brief memory of a horror movie with something evil lurking in the maize fields around a farm, came to Winter's mind. There was no time for that. He needed to focus on finding Matthew. He could be lying in one of the fields injured, or having suffered a heart attack. The other alternative, that he'd taken his own life, also came to his mind.

Vicky raised her hand in greeting to Gill up ahead and the worry on the other woman's face soon came into focus.

'He's never this long and I've never seen the dogs acting like this. They wanted me to follow them, look. It's as though they're leading us to him.'

Winter looked – she was right. Both dogs were pacing, looking at her, and then taking a few steps into the field of maize in front of them. One of them barked, impatient at their pace.

'Let's go,' Winter said, deliberately placing himself in the front of the two women and Daniel, and behind the dogs. If this turned out to be a crime scene, he wanted to be ready to react. He'd also rather spare the family from seeing a scene that might turn out to be horrific.

The dogs were fast, running on ahead and circling back when their human followers were too slow. Winter found himself almost jogging. From the original path they'd taken, the field of maize looked impenetrable, but along the path to the right that they were now following, you could see clearly all the way down each individual row. If Matthew was in the maize, they'd see him. Nobody spoke. There was just the panting of the dogs and the puffing in and out as the four of them made their way up the field.

Halfway along, the dogs darted down into the maize, leaving the main footpath.

Winter turned round. 'I'm going to ask you all to stay here a moment. Let me go first.'

Three pale faces had looked back at him. He wasn't sure they'd comply and so he turned around quickly to go and see where the dogs had gone and what may have befallen Matthew, before they changed their minds. Down the narrow channel between the maize plants, he could see the two dogs sniffing and pawing at a figure on the ground. Winter rushed straight in, looking carefully where he trod, but eager to see if there was anything medically he could do to help Matthew. One of the dogs was licking around his head and as Winter got closer he could see that there was unlikely to be anything anybody could do to help Matthew Cabot. But he needed to check anyway, carefully walking around the prone body where he could reach down to feel a pulse on the outstretched hand. Could Matthew have done this himself? Wracked by guilt at killing his brother perhaps? Winter couldn't see a gun, but he might possibly have fallen over one and covered it.

As Winter got closer and saw the big pool of sticky red blood that had flowed onto the earth, it was clear that not only was Matthew Cabot dead, it wasn't self-inflicted. Winter looked at the scene in front of him. It was the same style of killing as with Paul, the shot to the back of the head. The difference was that Matthew looked as though he'd been standing or running away, he certainly wasn't kneeling.

'Oh my god, Matthew!' Gill had walked down between the maize and was a few feet away, staring at her husband's body, the dog leads she'd been holding now lying on the ground like curled up snakes. She swayed and looked as if she was about to faint so Winter rushed back to her, supporting her arms and turning her around back towards where Vicky had blocked Daniel from going any further at the start of the maize channel.

'I'm so sorry, Mrs Cabot.' He walked her away, and then spoke to Vicky. 'Can you find somewhere to sit her down?'

'What's happened? Was that Matthew?' Vicky asked.

'Yes, I'm afraid he's dead. I'm going to call for assistance as soon as I've put the dogs on leads.'

'I can get them,' Daniel volunteered.

'No,' Winter said and then realised he'd been quite abrupt. 'You stay here and look after your aunt. This is a crime scene and I don't want anyone going down there unless absolutely necessary.'

Daniel didn't reply, but Winter was hardly surprised that the young man was lost for words. Winter didn't want him down there for two reasons: firstly out of humanity – the lad didn't need to see his uncle like that – and secondly because he was a potential suspect. It would be a great way to explain his fingerprints and DNA, if he'd gone back to the scene of the crime.

Winter retraced his steps, picking up the fallen leads and hoping that the dogs wouldn't protest at being dragged away from their dead master. The first one was easy, it had lain down next to Matthew, head on paws, nose right by his hand. Winter clipped the lead on no problem. The second one, which looked to be the younger of the two, wasn't so keen. It kept darting away each time he reached out for its collar, but in the end its dedication to its owner was also its downfall because it never darted far and eventually Winter had them both and was able to walk them away.

Vicky and Gill were both hugging each other and sobbing. Daniel stood there, hands hanging by his sides.

'Daniel, I need your help please,' Winter said, walking up to him. 'Can you keep a firm hold of the dogs? I don't want them going back to your uncle.'

Daniel had nodded and then crouched down to the two dogs, pulling them to him.

Winter walked away from them, taking his mobile from his pocket, and dialled the office. It was picked up immediately.

'DI Labey, what the hell do you think you're doing, you're about to let Joshua Redpath walk free and have gone behind my back?' The phone had been picked up by DCI Sharpe, who it was clear had been spoken to by the chief officer. 'That man in all likelihood killed Paul Cabot and you're just going to let him out? Do you know how much flack we are getting from the government and the public? Is it going to take another politician's death before you listen to me?'

Winter didn't give him the satisfaction of an argument – he already had the trump card. 'I need a forensic team and officer back-up. Matthew Cabot has been murdered. I'm on scene. I'm sure you also appreciate that Joshua Redpath is still in our custody suite and therefore can't be held responsible.'

There was a noise as the phone was transferred by hand to someone else.

'Sir.' It was Jonno's voice.

Winter repeated his request.

'No problem, I'll get that organised right away.' Then Jonno dropped his voice. 'Sorry about that, he was tearing a strip off me about Redpath as you rang and saw it was your number, snatched the phone.'

'That's fine, just wish I'd been there to see the look on his face when I told him how wrong he was.'

'It was a combination of a bird choking on a mouse, and a bulldog chewing on a wasp,' Jonno replied, 'make a great meme.'

Winter allowed himself a small smirk, but his professionalism kicked in and both of them switched back into business mode. 'We're in the maize field that's in-between the Cabot houses, closest one to Paul and Vicky's.' He gave a few more instructions and then returned his attention to the remaining family.

'Who is doing this?' Vicky asked him as he turned around and approached them.

'Why would anyone want both Paul and Matthew dead?'

Winter took a deep breath. 'I can't answer that right now. We need to first determine if the deaths are definitely connected.'

'Connected? Of course they must be, two brothers in one week.' Gill had dissolved into tears again and Vicky was forced to concentrate on comforting her sister-in-law.

Winter stayed with them in the field, until the forensic team had arrived and he could leave the body. Then he helped walk Gill back to her house. She was shaking and so Daniel supported her one side, with him on the other, and Vicky took the dogs.

He needed to speak to these three and then to Tom and George, see what they had been doing this morning. One of those five people had to be the killer. While he waited for his team to get in place and for the shock to ease in Gill and the others, he'd texted Saskia. *Matthew Cabot found murdered.*

She replied back immediately. *Shall I come over?*

If you can, could be helpful. I need to talk to all the remaining five suspects again.

Winter was taking a break from the heavy atmosphere in the house, when Saskia arrived on her bike. He was standing staring out across the maize fields where the forensic team were working to record everything they could. She pulled up next to him and took off her helmet, shaking her hair free like she did. That was another thing he liked and needed to get over.

'Thanks for coming,' he said to her.

'No problem, any indications as to what happened?'

'Matthew took their dogs out for a walk in the fields and didn't come back. We found him in the maize field, shot through the head like his brother, although he wasn't kneeling. Looked like he had tried to run.'

'Any ideas of the murder weapon?'

'Not yet. Someone has gone to check at Vicky and Paul's house, see if all the guns are still there, and Gill was going to find the combination to their safe to check Matthew's guns. Both Vicky and Daniel are in the house with her.'

'Well this definitely discounts the political motive,' Saskia said to him.

'Yeah, but we kind of knew that anyway, didn't we? We're still no closer to catching the killer.'

There was silence for a few moments and Winter wondered if maybe he'd been a bit harsh with his answer.

'Why were there two farm houses built?' Saskia suddenly said to him.

He turned to look at her. From where they were standing, they could just about see Paul and Vicky's house across the fields and she was looking between the two.

'If you own the land and that house, why would you build another farmhouse? It's not quite as large, but it's certainly set up as though it's an independent holding, with the gate and outbuildings. Surely if it was just for workers they'd just have built a row of cottages?'

Winter considered her question. 'Most of the farms in Jersey were very small. In the 1930s, before the war, there was something like 1,800 individual farms across the island and they didn't have huge swathes of land. I guess the grandfather bought this and the land at some point which is how he was able to create such a large farm,'

'Is that when it was built?' Saskia nodded towards the granite arch that led into the farm. Across the top was a piece of granite with the initials *HGLF 1891 MAB*. 'What are the letters for?'

'That's a date stone or marriage stone. Yes it could have been when it was built, although sometimes stones get put into buildings after they've been constructed, usually when they're modified. That would have been the initials of the couple the house was built for, or owned by at that time.'

'When was the other house built, do you know?'

'I don't but it might have a date stone too, but I'm not sure how that connects to our murders, especially if we think it's connected to the war.' Winter looked at her quizzically.

'I'm not sure, just seemed odd that the family had two houses, that's all. Sorry.'

Again, Winter felt as if maybe he'd been a bit short with her unnecessarily. Was he behaving like this because he felt rejected after last night, or because he was stressed about having just discovered a second murder victim? Either way, it was unacceptable, she was here to help him, the least he could do was be polite.

'Let's go and take a look at the crime scene,' he said to distract their conversation, and set off towards the entrance to the field where he knew the remains of Matthew Cabot still lay.

THIRTY
SATURDAY

Saskia hadn't been expecting a phone call that morning, least of all that there would be another murder. Part of her was pleased about the fact she could spend some more time with Winter, but the practical part of her was wishing she could take a break from him. She needed to get over her crush, a relationship was totally unrealistic. Either way, when she arrived, it seemed like he might feel the same way about needing a break, because he was a little short with her. Very unlike him. Of course, it could have just been the stress of the investigation.

She was glad to put her mind to something other than worrying whether or not David had committed murder. He was coming round later to talk to her and she'd played through the questions she would ask him, a thousand times in her head. Surely her brother wouldn't have gone so far off the rails? She'd have seen the signs... wouldn't she?

Viewing the crime scene would mean her second violent death in less than a week. This was becoming a habit she could quite happily do without. Saskia followed Winter's broad back up the field towards where she could see white coveralled forensic workers.

The day was getting more muggy and humid with every passing hour. The Jersey Met had forecast thunder and heavy showers later. Saskia hoped they'd arrive soon and clear the air.

'We think the victim ran down the field towards the house and then darted into the maize field,' Winter said to Saskia as they approached.

'So he's recognised the danger,' she replied. 'I wonder if that's because it was obvious, the killer had a gun pointing at him, or they'd told him, or because he'd guessed.'

'Well, if he guessed, he didn't tell us,' Winter replied. 'I'll ask Gill later, although I'd have thought that if he'd told her, she would have mentioned it after we found Matthew.'

'Unless it was her who he suspected and who killed him,' Saskia added.

Winter grunted and nodded. 'She'd have to be a pretty convincing actress if that is the case.'

'We've got a couple of them at La Moye,' Saskia said to him. 'They understand how to turn on the emotions as and when required.'

'He had the dogs with him too,' Winter said, thinking aloud. 'If you were a stranger, you might be worried about them attacking you. They're two big Labradors. But if you knew the dogs and they knew you, there would be nothing to worry about.'

The pair of them looked at each other.

'Especially if you started running away, the dogs would pick up on the anxiety but might not know that the person chasing you was the danger.'

'Right, let's get talking to them all,' Winter said.

Saskia could tell he was getting fed up with going around in circles. She had to jog to keep up with him.

. . .

They took over the dining room in Gill and Matthew Cabot's house, calling Vicky in first. She was quiet. That wasn't a surprise given that her own husband had been murdered just a few days previously, and now her brother-in-law.

'Can I ask you what you were doing this morning before I arrived?' Winter asked her.

She stared at him for a few moments and Saskia thought she wasn't going to reply.

'I don't know really. I got up quite early. I couldn't sleep, and I was looking through some photographs and at some cards that had arrived yesterday but I'd not opened them. Then Gill rang.'

Saskia studied her, trying to see if she was being evasive, or was simply still in shock.

'Were you close with your brother-in-law?'

'Matthew? Yes, he was always coming over to see Paul and the whole family get together for all big occasions. They only live across the fields, I mean, we occasionally had fall-outs, but never anything serious.'

'Did you see anyone this morning, or did anyone come to visit?'

'No. Not until you arrived.'

'What time did Daniel get up?'

'I didn't see him until he came down the stairs when you were there. He'd been having a lie in. The last few days have been exhausting for us all.'

'On the night of the election, can you remember exactly who was still at your house and where they were when you went up to bed?'

'Yes, I've already told you this: Paul obviously, Daniel, Tom, George, Joshua and Frank.'

'And where were they all?'

'Well, Joshua had just told me about Paul and his wife. We were in the dining room and I think he returned to the sitting room with the others. I didn't go in to check, but I think that everyone else was in there.'

'Did you hear what time Daniel came up to bed?'

'I was upset, DI Labey, I have to be honest – I wasn't paying attention to the clock, but I think it was about half an hour or so later.'

'And did you hear Joshua go into the spare room?'

'No. After I heard Daniel come up, I washed my face and got into bed, just in case he came in to say goodnight. I didn't want him to see that I'd been crying. I think I was probably asleep by the time Joshua came upstairs.'

'Did Daniel come in?'

'No.'

'And you heard nobody else coming and going?'

'Nothing. It had been a very long day, I'd had a few glasses of champagne. I was out cold.'

Daniel was next on Winter's list. Saskia sat quietly at the table, letting him lead. In all honesty, she wouldn't have had any choice in the matter anyway, he was on a roll.

'What were you doing this morning before I arrived?' Winter asked Daniel.

'Sleeping. I heard a bang, that woke me up and then a bit later I heard the phone ringing and you knocking, so I got up to see what was going on.'

'On the night of the election, can you tell me who was still up at your house when you went to bed, and where they all were?'

'Where they were?'

'Yes, what rooms they were in.'

'Oh, sure. It was Dad, me, Tom, George, Joshua, and Frank. My uncle had told me that Dad was planning on selling the farm to Frank and I'd asked to speak to Dad in his office. He apologised and said it had been a stupid idea and that he'd stop it.'

'Did you believe him?'

'I don't know. I guess, but I was just really upset that he'd even considered it.'

'The others were in the sitting room?'

'Frank, George, and Joshua were. Tom had come back from having got the port. Dad had asked me but I got Tom to do it because I wanted to talk to Dad after what Uncle Matthew had told me about Frank. They were all in the sitting room and they drank the port when Dad finished talking to me. I went upstairs to bed, but I heard them all toasting him and saying how good the port was. Mum had already gone up.'

'Once upstairs, did you hear anybody else come up?'

'No. I put my headphones on and listened to music to calm me down, then went to sleep.'

'And you heard nothing more that night?'

Daniel shook his head.

Winter let out a big sigh when Daniel left the room. Same stories as before. There was no guarantee that any of the other party guests had left the property. They could have hidden in the house or in one of the outbuildings and come back in. The doors would have been unlocked.

'What about Tom, he was downstairs in the sitting room. Wouldn't he have heard something?' Saskia asked.

'Not necessarily, no.' Winter replied. 'Any intruder could have come in the front or back door and not needed to go near the sitting room. Or they could have hidden in the adjoining cottage, or even upstairs and then appeared when Paul was alone. He was the last one up by all accounts. But we need to speak to Tom again, and George. I want to hear if either of them have alibis for this morning.'

.   .   .

Tom lived in Red Houses, less than a ten-minute drive from the farm. His flat was in a block of social housing not far from the small shopping precinct off the main road.

When he opened his door to them, he looked surprised.

'Is everything alright?' He asked, scanning Winter's face.

'Would it be OK to come in for a quick chat?' Winter asked him.

There was a slight hesitation as Tom's brain clearly ran through all the possibilities of why DI Labey and Saskia were there, and then he opened the door.

'Sure, of course. Come on in. I've not been long up though, so please excuse the mess. I thought I'd answered all the questions the other day.'

'You've been here all morning?' DI Labey asked, looking around the flat.

Saskia did the same. It was a classic bachelor pad: all dark colours and a little bit dusty.

'Yes. Why you asking me that?' Tom had been clearing a space for them on the sofa, moving some clothes and what looked to have been a bowl of breakfast cereal.

'I'm sorry to inform you that Matthew Cabot was found dead this morning and we are treating his death as suspicious.'

'Matthew? You're kidding!'

'No.'

'Shit! Poor Gill,' Tom replied and sat himself down on the armchair.

'You understand that I need to ask you where you were this morning.'

'Where I was?' Tom looked at Winter. 'Here. I told you, I got up late.'

'Can you tell me what time?'

'About an hour and a half ago if you must know. Sat and

watched TV while I ate my breakfast.' Tom nodded to the empty bowl of cereal. 'I've not been sleeping well since Paul died. It's been a big shock. We'd known each other since nursery school. We were like brothers.'

'Did you go to the same boarding school in England as Paul and George?'

Tom shook his head. 'No. I stayed in the island. Went to the local state school, Les Quennevais, but we never lost touch.'

'On the night of the election, what time did you go to bed?'

'Well, I didn't exactly go to bed, more like crashed out on the sofa. It was all the champagne and port. Can't do booze like I used to. Joshua went up to bed and Frank and George had left. Paul and I carried on talking for a bit and then I think I must have just fallen asleep. Next thing I knew Vicky was collecting glasses in the morning and then I heard her gasp when she went into Paul's study and so I got up to see if she was OK. That's when I saw the picture. Not long after that, you came round.'

'So, you heard nobody else coming and going?'

'No, sorry. I did say that before in my statement. I'd had a belly full of booze. I was out cold.'

'Were you aware that Matthew told Daniel about Frank's plans for the farm?'

'Frank's plans? What do you mean? I saw Daniel speaking to Paul, he'd looked a bit upset, and then later Paul asked Frank if he could have a word. I vaguely remember that, but that's it.'

'But Paul seemed fine to you, up until you went to sleep?'

'Yeah absolutely, he'd been on good form. He'd just won the election. What plans? What does Frank have to do with it?'

'He wanted to buy the farm and redevelop it.'

Tom's face hardened. 'Really! Well no, I didn't know. Paul didn't tell me that. No wonder Daniel was upset. Had he signed the contracts?'

'No, it didn't get that far. He called it off, that's why Frank left.'

Tom huffed and shook his head, turning away from them. 'That's surprised me.'

Saskia could see he was genuinely floored by that revelation.

'You're good friends. Are you more surprised that he hadn't told you, or that he was doing it?' she interjected.

Tom looked at her. 'Both.'

'How friendly were you with Matthew?'

'Well, I've known him pretty much all his life too. He's four years younger than Paul and I. I'd count Matthew and Gill as friends. My family has lived round here for generations and so we've all known the Cabots for years.'

'And there's nobody you can think of who would want to harm them?'

Tom shook his head.

'What about your parents? Would they know of anyone?'

'I'm afraid they're both gone. It's just me now. That's them in the photographs over there.' Tom nodded to a collection of photographs on the wall of the corridor which led to the front door.

'OK, thank you for your time,' Winter said as he headed towards the exit.

He stopped and looked at the photographs on his way out and Saskia did the same. There were black and white shots of a hard-working Jersey couple standing either side of a cow.

'That's my great-grandparents,' Tom said, 'and that's my grandparents.' There was another photograph, this time inside a house. A young couple standing together with various food items on the kitchen table and a small painting of a Jersey cow behind them. It looked pre Second World War and it must have been some kind of celebration. 'My grandfather died in the war. He'd volunteered for the army.'

'Did your grandmother stay here?'

'No. My dad was very young. She thought she might be able

to keep in contact with my grandad easier if she was in England and she was worried about my father staying here, so close to the war in Europe. They got off on the last boat. My great-grandmother stayed, though.'

'Hard times,' Winter said sympathetically.

'Yes. Although despite him sacrificing his life in the war, some accused them of cowardice for evacuating.'

'Your parents?' Winter asked, pointing at another photograph, in colour this time, of a couple with nineties-style clothes and hair. They were in a small house with a little white dog at their feet.

'Yes,' Tom replied. 'Dad came back after Liberation, with my grandmother, and married Mum, another Jersey girl. My gran never remarried.'

Saskia wondered why Tom had never found a wife himself, but then decided that the pot couldn't really call the kettle black. Lots of people had good reasons for being on their own.

They thanked him and left. Still no closer to finding their killer.

George was clearly surprised when Winter and Saskia knocked on his door again.

'I thought I'd answered all your questions,' he said to them both. 'I'm afraid I have to go out shortly.'

Saskia thought he looked smarter and more positive than he'd been on their last visit.

'We will only keep you a few minutes.' Winter smiled at George. 'I promise.'

He hesitated, but opened the front door fully and let them follow him through to the kitchen. A motorbike helmet was on the kitchen table.

'You have a motorbike?' Winter said to him surprised.

'Yes. What's wrong with that?' George replied defensively.

'I am allowed to, I have my licence if you want to check. I was only suspended for a year.'

'No, it's fine,' Winter replied, trying to appease him.

'So?' George said. He was clearly irritated by their presence.

'So,' Winter replied, 'Matthew Cabot has been found dead in suspicious circumstances this morning.'

'Matthew!' George repeated. 'Bloody hell!'

'We have to ask you, what you were doing this morning?'

'Me? Why me?' George looked from one to the other of them. 'Oh I get it, the prime suspect is the nutter, the one who has mental health problems. That's innovative, DI Labey.'

'No. That's not why I'm asking you. We've asked everyone who was there last Wednesday night.'

George sighed deeply. 'I was here. Alone. I spoke to a friend on the telephone about an hour ago. We arranged to go out later this morning, hence why I need to leave shortly.'

'How well did you know Matthew?'

'Not that well. He'd come round Paul's house occasionally when I was there, and of course he was there on Wednesday night. I have no reason to want the man dead, if that's what you're asking. And now I'm afraid I really am going to have to ask you to leave as I'm going to be late.' George looked at his watch.

Winter hesitated a moment and Saskia thought he was weighing up whether to ask another question.

'OK, thank you for your time, Mr Sanchez, we don't want to hold you up any longer,' Winter said, walking back out of the kitchen. Saskia followed. She could tell Winter was annoyed by George's attitude.

'Well, he wasn't quite as pleasant as last time we visited!' Winter said as he flopped down into the car seat. 'Are you sure he's not got multiple personalities? That was a whole different side to him.'

'He was in a bad mood that we'd turned up when he was going out,' Saskia said. Right on cue, George walked out of his front door with his bike helmet on, glaring over at them still sitting in his drive. They watched as he got on his bike and rode away.

'Didn't tell us about the motorbike either, did he? We thought he didn't have any transport because he'd lost his licence.'

'Economical with the truth, I think they call it,' Saskia said.

'Well that means he could have ridden back to the Cabot house after being dropped off at home by the taxi. How do we know if anything George Sanchez has told us is real?'

THIRTY-ONE

SATURDAY

Saskia wasn't entirely sure how she managed to focus at all during the day's investigation into Matthew Cabot's death. Every time she looked at Winter, she was reminded that he could at any moment be investigating the murder of Allan Hall. A murder her brother might have committed.

When she got home, she'd resumed her pacing up and down until she heard David's car pull up outside. She had to remember her training, keep this professional. If she ambushed him the second he walked through the door then she'd get nothing out of him.

'Can't stay long,' David said as he sauntered into her cottage. 'Lots going on at home.'

'Do you not want a drink?' Saskia asked, noting what he'd said.

'Not for me.'

'So how has your week been?' Saskia wondered if David would mention the police coming round, or just ignore it.

'Yeah, alright.'

'Has Allan turned up?' She fished for his reaction.

'Yeah. Dead. They pulled him out the sea apparently.'

'Oh my word, Jackie must be upset.'

'She was.'

Saskia saw a thought cross David's mind.

'You know I don't understand people, especially you women,' he said, completely changing the subject in his usual self-centred way. 'A few of her friends came round for some lunch today, just a relaxed thing. I went to the gym, but when I came back they were all watching this video of a girl acting. They showed it to me and said, "What do you think, isn't she marvellous?" I watched it and she was rubbish. Really wooden, mediocre, so I told them that. Jackie had a go at me and they looked upset. So tell me, why do people ask my opinion if they don't actually want to hear the answer? The truth? People say that psychopaths are bad, but it's everyone else that lies all the time and thinks it's OK.'

'What did Jackie say?'

'She said it had been one of her friend's daughters and I should have been polite and positive. But that's just lying. So, you tell me why that's right. Now, she reckons I'm "on the spectrum" or something because I tell it like it is. The spectrum means autistic, right?'

'Yes,' Saskia replied. Usually she'd have found that quite amusing, but today she had other things on her mind. 'People like to hear positive feedback to encourage them. It's not so much lying, as being encouraging.'

'Don't get it.' David shrugged.

'Do you know what happened to Allan?' Saskia asked him, watching closely.

'Allan?' David asked as though surprised she was even thinking about him. 'Kevin killed him.'

'Kevin, his boyfriend?'

'Yeah.'

Saskia looked at David, who was studying his fingernails.

'Why? Why would Kevin hurt him?'

'I heard them arguing. Kevin came round later, Allan disappears.' David looked up at her and shrugged his shoulders as though amazed she couldn't see the connection.

'And the police agree with that?' she asked, hopefully.

'They're investigating, but they know about the argument and stuff.'

'David, did you hurt Allan? Please tell me if you have because I might be able to help you.'

'How could you help me if I'd killed him, Sas?' He gave her one of his innocent, butter-wouldn't-melt faces that reminded her of when he was little. 'I know that you're the reason why I've managed to keep out of trouble. If it wasn't for you I'd have been in prison years ago. You show me how I need to behave. You've always done that. Right back to when we were at school and that teacher showed me up in front of the whole playground. If it hadn't been for you I'd have hit him with that brick and that would have been a downward spiral.'

'I haven't always managed to curb you...' Saskia said to him, her eyes narrowed.

'No. OK, occasionally I've slipped up, usually when you weren't around. But you are here, we have these chats and they're good. Why would I have hurt Allan? I'm happy living here with Jackie, why endanger that?'

'It could get really awkward for me if there's any suspicion,' Saskia added, 'because the police detective who came round to see you yesterday, is the same one I work with sometimes.'

'Him?' David shrugged. 'There's nothing to worry about. I'm not going to risk everything we've built up, not for some ex-con who drives cars around for a living.' He looked at her, almost challenging her to prove otherwise. 'Anyway, I need to head off, gotta go out soon.'

Saskia watched him walk out the door. Everything he'd said had made sense – why would he risk everything? Perhaps it *had* been a domestic. Domestic violence and murder against men was more common than most people thought, partly because they were even more reluctant than women to tell someone about the abuse. Perhaps David was telling the truth and she was just being paranoid. One way or another, she'd find out in the next few days as Winter began to investigate Allan's murder.

* * *

David walked down the path, waiting to see if the annoying dog from next door came out to bark at him. It did. He'd had enough of its high-pitched yapping. When he got to the end of the wall, he looked back at the neighbour's house to check she wasn't there, and then discreetly opened the latch on her gate. It didn't open straight away, but that was good. He needed to get in his car first.

David got into the driver's seat and turned the engine on, and waited. At some point the bloody dog was bound to be nosey and push at the gate and walk out. Then bang. He'd have him.

He felt a surge of something running through his blood-stream – there it was again, that buzz he'd got from killing Allan. Nowhere near as high, but it was still there. Shutting this damned dog up would be a victory.

David waited, and then leant out the car window and made what he thought would be a suitable noise to attract a dog. He watched and saw the wooden gate move a little as though something was pushing against it. Then there was a nose and the little hairy mutt stuck its head out, nose to the ground. It must have sensed him, or smelt him, because it looked up in his direction, coming fully out of the garden and then starting to yap at him.

David put his foot down on the accelerator and pointed the

car straight at the dog which was by now standing nearly in the middle of the lane.

As he accelerated, he didn't take his eyes off it. Any second now and he'd be on top of it and it would be nothing but blood and smashed bone.

He was just about to reach it when it moved. Sensing danger, it darted towards the gate which had stayed slightly ajar.

David swerved towards it to compensate and ensure he hit it.

There was a sickening bump and then a scraping as his front wing hit the little granite wall and scraped along it.

Shit! Had he got it?

David stopped the car and got out, looking back the way he'd come, hoping to see a squashed piece of fur.

Nothing.

Then it started barking again.

'Pushki, Pushki!' The irritating old woman came rushing out into her garden, and was joined by Saskia, alerted to the incident by the noise. 'What happened?' the old lady asked, hugging the dog to her.

David looked at Saskia's horrified face.

'I had to swerve to avoid him,' David said to them both. 'He was in the road.'

'Oh my word, my poor baby,' the old woman said. 'The gate must have not been closed properly. Thank god you missed him. But what about your car?'

David walked round to the side of his car and looked at the grey scrape down the front left wing. He felt the anger bubble in his veins and he gritted his teeth. 'It will be fine, it's nothing serious,' he said, looking at Saskia.

'But it's damaged...' the old woman continued.

'It's fine. The insurance will cover it. Don't you worry,' David said, walking up to her and smiling. 'And you, little fellow, are lucky,' he said, addressing the dog. 'You get to live to see another day.'

'Thank you so much,' the old woman said, 'I'm going to have to get that gate fixed.'

David got back in his car, swore, and drove off. The dog might have been lucky this time, but its luck would run out eventually.

THIRTY-TWO

SATURDAY

Jonno, or Detective Sergeant Jonathan Vibert, was still in the office when Winter got back from his interviews. He and Jonno were good friends, harking back to their school days, but Winter also rated him as a thorough detective. Jonno was exhibits officer again, keeping records of all the evidence that was coming in.

'How's it going?' he said to Jonno as he walked up to his desk. 'Fancy a coffee or something to eat? I'm just going to the canteen.'

'A coffee would be grand, mate, thanks.' Jonno smiled at his friend. 'And a Mars Bar too, keep me going. Although they've got so bloody small nowadays I'm not sure it will even touch the sides.'

'All our favourites have got smaller since we were kids. A bit like the days have got shorter. It's a government conspiracy to squeeze more taxes out of us,' Winter joked. 'So, what you working on?'

Jonno leant back and let Winter get a better look at his screen. 'Cross-checking the clothes we got back from Forensics with the photos from election night.'

'I thought that had already been done?'

'It has, but not by me and I want to put my mind at rest. We know that the most likely killer was one of those in the house already, and yet all the clothes we got from them have been clean.'

'Who've you checked so far?'

'Redpath. He was the one who had the best opportunity to switch something out when he got home.'

'I take it nothing.'

'Nope. They're looking like the same threads to me. I'm just double-checking Tom Le Feuvre's now.'

'But he didn't leave.'

'So he says,' Jonno replied, turning back to his screen. 'He was wearing a white T-shirt and jeans. Easily swapped.'

Winter left Jonno to it and walked to the canteen, but his mind was no longer on food and drink. Jonno was right, and there were a couple of other things which were niggling him. Something that Saskia had said to him yesterday came into his mind. The thoughts were clearly distracting him more than he realised because instead of taking him to the canteen, his legs had carried him downstairs on autopilot. Winter took that as an omen and went straight to his car. He'd make it up to Jonno, but, right now, he needed to go and check something out at Paul and Vicky Cabot's house.

The more he went down the line of thinking that had suddenly opened up to him, the more concerned he became. Winter put his lights on and headed for the Noirmont Point area as fast as he could. If he was right, then another life could depend on it.

As he pulled into the yard at the house. The place looked quiet and calm. Perhaps nobody was at home – they might be over at Gill's still coming to terms with Matthew's death. He parked the car round the side of the house where it wasn't so obvious and then went and knocked.

At first, there was no answer. He tried to peer in through the windows but couldn't see anyone. He knocked again and this time was rewarded by the sound of somebody coming down the stairs.

'Oh, it's you!' Daniel pulled the door open, his face falling at the sight of the detective.

'Is your mum in?' Winter asked.

'No, she's over at Gill's.'

'Can I come in?'

'I guess...' Daniel hesitated.

'I need your help, actually,' Winter said to the young lad. 'Could you show me where you get the port from?'

'The port?'

'Yes. On the night of the election, your dad asked you to go and get the family port to celebrate. Where is it kept?'

Daniel looked at him as though he'd lost his marbles. 'It's in Gran's cottage.'

'The dowager cottage next door?'

'Yeah, but we have an interlocking door—'

'I'd like to take a look please,' Winter said to Daniel firmly.

Winter followed Daniel to the door. He tried it, but it was locked.

'Mum must have locked it again, I'll need to get the key.'

'Why's that? Why's it locked?'

'Cos it's got Gran and Grandad's stuff in it, I guess. Dad insists it's kept locked. Gran's still alive you know, just not living here anymore.'

'I know officers and Forensics searched the cottage on the morning after the election, but I'm not sure if they went through this way.'

Daniel shrugged.

'Mum probably locked it up again after she found that stuff had been stolen from our house.'

'Where's the key kept?'

'In Dad's study,' Daniel replied and started walking towards the room.

The painting of Daniel's great-grandfather had been propped up to one side, the pieces gathered. Apart from that – and the gap on the wall where it had once hung – the study looked tidy and probably how it was supposed to look.

'He keeps it in his desk drawer,' Daniel said, going round to the other side of the desk and pulling open the drawer. He looked inside, moving a few things around, and then frowned. 'It should be back in here, that's where I got it from.'

Winter watched as Daniel pulled open a couple of other drawers and looked quickly through them. Then he looked up at him. 'It's not here. I can't find it.'

'Was it you who got the key on Wednesday evening?'

Daniel's forehead wrinkled. 'Yeah. Dad asked me and so I came and got the key, then I bumped into Dad in the hallway. It was the first time he'd been on his own since Uncle Matthew had told me about Frank Mason.' His face suddenly brightened. 'That's right, of course, I gave the key to Tom, asked him to get the port.'

'Did your dad know that you'd asked Tom?'

Daniel shook his head. 'No, I forgot about it, but he wouldn't have minded. Tom and him go way back.'

'And you and your dad were in here talking about Frank when Tom came back with the port?'

'I went upstairs, but I heard Tom in the sitting room with the others. He must still have the key, or maybe he left it in the door and Mum's not put it back. It's all been a bit of a blur.'

'Is there another key?' Winter said to him, a thousand thoughts racing through his mind.

'I don't think so. No. Dad had the only one.'

'Do you have a screwdriver?'

'A screwdriver?'

'Yes. I'm going to have to force the lock.'

'You can't do that,' Daniel said, his face aghast.

'I need to do it, Daniel. I think that what's behind that door could help us understand why your father and Uncle Matthew were killed.'

'What? It's just Gran and Grandad's place,' Daniel replied.

'Please, will you trust me on this? The house is technically yours, it's your property, so will you give me permission to go in there so I can find the answers for you all?'

Daniel stared at him for what seemed like an age. Winter could see the lad's mind weighing up the options, afraid in case he might get into trouble, and yet realising that it was his decision to make.

'OK, but will you get it fixed after?'

'We can get a locksmith out if needs be, yes.'

Daniel gave a slight nod. 'I know where Dad keeps his screwdrivers, hold on.'

Winter paced up and down the hall, eager to get beyond the wooden door. It wasn't long before Daniel came running with a tool kit.

'Ah, good lad,' Winter said, choosing one that looked like it would do the job.

It was an old lock, but sturdy, so it took a few minutes, but he did it. Winter pushed the handle down and the door opened.

The room smelt a little musty, the kind of smell you get in an old building when it hasn't been used and the air has stayed still and the damp crept into the structure.

Daniel flicked a switch on the right-hand side and a sitting room was lit up.

'Their bedroom is up those stairs, and that's the kitchen,' Daniel said, pointing to an alcove through which Winter could see worktops and a cooker. The room was filled with photographs and paintings, ornaments and books, many dating back to the war and beyond.

'Where's the port kept?' He asked Daniel.

'Over there in that cupboard.'

'How would Tom have known that?'

'Uhh... good point, I don't know. I guess he'd have just searched for it? No wait, I said to him it was in the cupboard by the TV.'

'But there are two cupboards by the TV.'

Daniel looked towards the television. 'The port's in that one,' he said, 'the one on the right.'

Winter walked over to the cupboard on the left and pulled the door open. Inside it was crammed full of more paintings, photographs, books and ceramics. Even a bit of silver was in there. But there was one painting in particular which caught Winter's eye. It was another clue that confirmed his growing suspicion. Winter looked at the books that were piled up: they were handwritten diaries and they looked as though they'd been recently disturbed. Everything else was neatly stacked, but these were shoved back in haphazardly. He pulled one out and sat down to flick through it.

'I've got to go,' Daniel said, 'I promised Mum and Gill that I'd walk the dogs,' Daniel said to him.

'You just going across to the other house?' Winter asked him.

Daniel nodded.

'OK. I'll be across soon too.' He turned back to the diaries, which were dated 1944. The handwriting was small, difficult to read, but as he flicked through the pages, it became blatantly clear what had been recorded.

His mobile ringing made him physically jump.

'Jonno,' he said, 'you nearly gave me a bloody heart attack.'

'Yeah well, I've died of thirst and lack of sugar, mate. What happened to the coffee and Mars bar?'

'Sorry, I'm following something up.'

'Well, you might want to follow this up. I found a photograph of Tom Le Feuvre on election night, clothes look the same alright, but it's the trainers which are different. The ones he wore in the photos have a gold strip on them. The ones we have in evidence do not.'

'Right, I want him arrested. I've just found some evidence here at Paul Cabot's house which gives Tom his motive. He must have gone back to his flat after killing Paul, changed and then come back here to make it look like he never left. Search the flats and where he works for any possible incineration points. And if you find anything, see if there is a metal key in amongst the ash, would you? The jeans he was wearing on the night probably had a key in the pocket.'

'On it,' Jonno said, and the line went dead.

How could he have been so blind, it was there all along. The question that he'd dismissed yesterday from Saskia about the two houses, and even the date stone, it was there for all to see. The smashed painting with only Vicky and Tom's fingerprints. He'd gone back in the morning after and moved the frame so that gave a reason for his prints being there. He'd probably slashed it when he came back from killing Paul the night before. Then there was the access to the gun safe. Tom would have known the combination because Vicky said it was their wedding date. Paul would have gone with his friend to the bunker, totally unaware of what he'd found out that night. The terrible secret that the Cabot's had hidden from Tom's family all those years. This was all about family revenge. Revenge for something which had happened eighty years ago.

Winter sighed for the millionth time at the futility of it all. Two deaths all because of one man's actions eighty years ago. He looked at his watch and a horrifying thought came to him. He jumped up from the chair and ran from the cottage and out of the house. He had to get to the other farmhouse. Daniel was the only one left.

Winter got back on his mobile as he ran up the path. It

would be quicker than driving and he might be able to intercept Daniel as he took the dogs into the fields.

'Jonno, any luck?'

'Tom's not at home or work, we're trying to find out if there are any other addresses he might be at.'

'Get me back-up at both Cabot farmhouses,' he breathlessly shouted down the phone.

Vicky and Gill looked horrified as he burst into the kitchen where they were bent over something they were writing.

'Where's Daniel?' he blurted out.

'He's taken the dogs,' Vicky said. 'What's going on? What's the matter?'

'Any particular direction?' he gasped.

'The fields.'

'Stay here,' he ordered.

Winter didn't have time to explain to the two women; he ran straight back towards the fields and started scanning for any signs of the lad or the dogs. Perhaps he was overreacting, perhaps Daniel wasn't in any danger at all, but one thing Winter knew for sure was that he wasn't prepared to take that chance.

He ran up into the maize fields and thought he caught the sight of a flash of black. Was that one of the dogs? He headed towards it, still keeping his eyes alert for any other signs of life.

Winter ran up the field, muscles pumping and heart racing, the sound of voices drifting to him on the breeze. He slowed a moment, trying to keep his own breathing quieter so he could hear. As he turned a curve in the field and drew closer, the sound of the voices grew louder, clearer, amongst the maize. It was Tom, and his words were threatening. Daniel was pleading with him.

Winter texted Jonno, *Need armed support*, and sent a GPS location with it.

He had no weapons, no protection, not even a police radio. He was going to have to use his wits to make sure that nobody got harmed.

Winter was just weighing up his best move, when his position was given away by the dogs, who started to bark.

'What's that? Who's there?' Tom shouted.

There was nothing for it now but to show himself. Winter pushed the maize aside and walked up to Daniel and Tom, putting himself between the two of them as a shield.

He would have arrested Tom immediately, but for the shotgun that was currently pointed at his head.

'It's over, Tom,' Winter said. 'I've seen your great-grandmother's diaries. I know what Philippe Cabot did, but you can't blame an innocent eighteen-year-old boy for that. It's not going to achieve anything.'

'Isn't it?' Tom spat back. 'Do you have any idea how betrayed I felt? My best friend, my life-long mate, and he knew but never said anything. While she was here, alone, afraid, and in failing health during the Occupation years, Philippe forced my great-grandmother to hand over her farm to him for nothing. Feeding her lies, all for his own gain. The farm that she and my great-grandfather, Henry had built. She died thinking her family had abandoned her and there was no hope, that the Cabots were looking out for her, helping her, when all they were doing was taking everything.

'When my grandmother came back with my father, Philippe Cabot told her that the Germans had looted the place, taken all their belongings, and her mother-in-law had sold it to the Cabots. My grandmother was penniless, a single mother. My grandfather had fought for our freedom and died and the Cabots did nothing to help her, except to give her a job in the fields. *Our own fields*. And they always treated her and my father as second-class citizens because they'd evacuated and not stayed. We never had any money, I've always struggled, we couldn't afford the education that Paul had. He knew all that and yet he could still look me in the eyes and tell me he was my friend. Philippe may have had a great public image, but he behaved as badly as the Germans towards my family.'

'But even if you were upset at Paul, why kill Matthew?'

'He'd always looked down on our family for not staying in Jersey for the occupation, worshipped his bloody great-grandfather.'

There were tears streaming down Tom's face as he ranted, spittle coming out of his mouth. The barrel of the gun wavered, but it was still inches from Winter's head. He'd pushed Daniel behind him so that he completely shielded the boy. Winter had assessed the weapon: it was semi-automatic. That meant Tom would have more than one shot, perhaps a dozen or more. They weren't going to be able to dodge that many bullets.

'Daniel hasn't done anything,' Winter said gently. 'Let him get back to his mum.'

'No! He's inherited my farm, *my land*. My birthright. He's just continuing on the wrong that's been done.'

'Tom, it's eighty years ago, three generations on. Surely this has to stop now?'

Winter was coiled like a spring. In just a few seconds, everything he'd learnt in Krav Maga about disarming a threat had run through his mind. If Tom didn't lower the gun, he was ready.

'No. No, I'm sorry, DI Labey. Step aside or I'll have to shoot you too. I have to finish this.'

Adrenaline, training, and the sheer will to survive, all kicked in at once. Winter put his hands up surrendering, bringing them as close to the barrel of the gun as he could.

'Please, Tom, don't do this,' he said to him again, this time as though he was backing down.

The look on Tom's face told him that there was no reasoning with him.

Winter's right hand shot out, pushing the muzzle of the gun away from him and Daniel. Tom let off a round, then a second as he tried to bring it back towards them. Winter moved fast, kicking Tom straight in the chest, sending him flying backwards. The gun shot once again into the air. Before Tom could even catch the breath back in his lungs, Winter was on him, wrestling the gun from his hands and pinning his knees onto his torso to hold him down.

'Tom le Feuvre, I am arresting you on the suspicion of the murder of Paul Cabot and Matthew Cabot.' Winter threw the gun behind him and turned Tom over onto his stomach. He didn't have any handcuffs on him, so his only option was to keep sitting on the man until back-up arrived.

'DI Labey, stand up,' the voice came from behind him. 'I don't want to hurt you, please get off him.'

Winter twisted round to see Daniel Cabot pointing the rifle at them both.

'What are you doing, Daniel?' Winter said, exasperation in his voice.

'He killed my dad and my uncle.' Daniel's voice wavered with emotion.

'Put the gun down, Daniel. If you shoot him that's your life ruined, don't be stupid.'

'He was going to kill me, it was self-defence.'

'No it isn't because I'm a witness. Are you going to kill me too?' As soon as Winter said that, he regretted it. The boy was highly emotional – perhaps that was exactly what he'd do.

Winter twisted as much as he could without taking his weight off Tom and allowing him to escape.

'Think about your mum and your aunt, Daniel. They both need you. Put the gun down. This is over. He's going to spend the rest of his life in jail for what he's done. Don't make the same mistake.'

There was a sound and Winter flinched before he realised it wasn't a gunshot but a sob. A deep, gut-wrenching sob of grief. Daniel fell onto his knees on the ground, discarding the gun, and burying his face in his hands.

Winter felt the relief flow through him, but couldn't move to console the boy, not until Tom Le Feuvre was in handcuffs.

A couple of minutes later, they heard shouts down the field and Winter knew that back-up had arrived. He shouted out to his team that he had things under control. Tom made one last effort to escape but it was futile, he didn't have Winter's bulk and strength and was no match for his determination.

As his colleagues handcuffed Tom, Winter walked over to Daniel who was still sobbing on the ground, the two dogs sitting by his side.

'It's time to go home now, Daniel,' he said to him gently.

'Aren't you going to arrest me?' he asked, looking up at him.

'Arrest you? What for? Get up now, let's get you and these dogs back home. Your mum and aunt will be worried sick.'

THIRTY-THREE

FRIDAY, FIVE DAYS LATER

Saskia was free when she was riding the waves. No worries about David, no memories of her father shadowing her, no anxiety over whether Mark Byrne, the prison guard from work, was stalking her. When she surfed, Saskia could let herself go. It was just her and the sea, her board an extension of her body. Some days, she wished she could stay out on the waves forever. Never have to touch back on shore and face up to the realities of her life.

Today was not one of those days. Today she wasn't alone and it created a different feeling for her. Winter had turned up at the beach just as she was about to go in. She'd recognised his broad shoulders and muscular chest in his tight wetsuit, and there'd been a mix of both dread and delight. She loved being around him, having his company. But she knew that she loved it far too much to just be friends. Every time she saw him, she battled with the urge to just throw caution to the wind and be with him.

But not today. Today they were surfing companions, riding the waves until they turned and the swell dropped. Then they walked up to their cars, pulling their wetsuits off and hanging them over the railings on the top of the sea wall to drip.

'Might have a couple of cold beers and some Doritos in the boot.' Winter smiled at her. 'Fancy celebrating the end of another successful investigation?'

'Be rude not to.' She'd smiled back at him, and they'd headed back down to the beach where they could be alone. The warmth of the sea wall on their backs, the burning red sun starting its journey to the bottom of the sea in front of them.

Winter let out a big sigh, put a big handful of Doritos into his mouth and passed the packet to Saskia. 'Thanks again for all your work on the Cabot case,' he said in between crunches. 'You even pointed out the date stone with Tom's great-grandparents' initials on it, Henry George Le Feuvre and Marie-Anne Bennett. Can't believe that didn't make the penny drop.'

'Like we said, it was several generations ago and people just become blind to the history around them,' Saskia reassured him.

'They might forget, but they also need to learn to forgive too,' Winter added. 'Vicky and Daniel have. They've asked for the charges to be dropped against Joshua Redpath. The Redpaths are going to move back to England. A fresh start.'

'That's a good result for them,' Saskia said, not missing the pleasure in Winter's voice as he told her that. He had a good heart.

'Well, yet again you were spot on with your profiling. We're going to have to put you on the payroll soon.'

'Glad to help.' Saskia smiled at him. 'Could do with you stopping filling up my prison and giving me more work, though,' she joked. Tom Le Feuvre had arrived that week and she'd already interviewed him to assess any levels of risk to himself or others.

'Ah, sorry about that, we're about to send you another one too. We arrested the boyfriend of that man we found floating off

St Catherine's,' Winter said, putting another handful of Doritos in his mouth.

Saskia's heart jumped. So David had been telling the truth. She nearly burst with relief while she waited for Winter to finish his mouthful of crunching.

'So it was definitely murder?' she asked innocently.

'Yes, for sure. We had various bits of circumstantial evidence which pointed to him.' Winter put two more Doritos into his mouth.

Saskia closed her eyes and felt a wave of relaxation wash through her like a warm rinse.

'But the stolen necklace box hidden in his car, along with some traces of blood, are what will convict him. He can't explain those away.'

An icy grip pulled at Saskia's intestines. 'Necklace box?' she queried.

'Yeah, a fifty-grand necklace had been stolen from Jackie Slater the weekend Allan was murdered. The boyfriend had the box; it's got his fingerprints on it, but we've not found the necklace yet.'

A vision of the necklace that David had asked her to look after a couple of weeks ago, came into Saskia's mind. 'Fifty thousand, that's a lot of necklace...' she said to Winter, trying to keep her voice steady.

'Yeah, three big diamonds, bought it for herself for her birthday, would you believe? I buy myself a McDonald's if I'm lucky.' He crunched on more crisps.

Saskia's ears were ringing, her heart pounding. Back at her little cottage, in a tin in the cupboard in her bedroom, she'd hidden the diamond necklace that David had given her the morning he'd turned up and told her he'd bought it for Jackie's birthday. He'd asked Saskia to keep it safe so Jackie wouldn't find it. It had three big diamonds and no box.

Perhaps she had already known. Maybe she'd been kidding

herself that David hadn't killed Allan Hall and that he really was changing, buying expensive gifts for his girlfriend. Perhaps even starting to feel something for her. Settling down. Was that how her mother had thought in the early years with her father? Trying to fool herself that the psychopath in him would somehow disappear? Saskia had ignored the warning signs when David told her about the French client and the prawns in his brie sandwich which had very nearly killed him. She'd disregarded everything that her training and her experience had told her she needed to beware of.

Now, her brother was a murderer and she was an accessory for hiding stolen goods. And the police detective next to her, who she was falling in love with, couldn't learn about any of that. Ever.

A LETTER FROM THE AUTHOR

Dear reader,

Huge thanks for reading *Secrets in the Blood*. I hope you are enjoying spending time with Saskia, Winter, and even David! This is their second book and if you want to continue their journey with them, and join other readers in hearing about my new releases and bonus content, you can sign up here:

www.stormpublishing.co/gwyn-bennett

If you enjoyed this book and could spare a few moments to leave a review that would be hugely appreciated. Even a short review can make all the difference in encouraging a reader to discover my books for the first time. Thank you so much!

As *Secrets in the Blood* indicates, the Channel Islands were the only part of the British Isles to be occupied by the German forces during the Second World War. The British government made a strategic decision not to defend the isles as they felt the costs in terms of both local lives and servicemen would not have been justified. Only around a fifth of Jersey people evacuated before the invasion, the rest spent the war under German rule. That part of the story was true. The rest of it, including all the characters, isn't.

Everywhere you go in Jersey, its history is marked upon its landscape and so I'm really lucky to be able to use the unique locations within the stories I create and to combine them with my imagination.

Thank you again for reading this second book in the Saskia Monet series. If you would like to stay in touch with me and get a free novella as well as hear about special offers and all my other books, you can join my free readers' club at gwynbennett.com

You can also keep in touch with me and my publisher Storm on our social channels. You'll find me on Facebook and you can also follow me on Amazon.

Happy reading

Gwyn Bennett

www.amazon.com/author/gwynbennett

 facebook.com/GwynGBwriter
instagram.com/gwyngb

ACKNOWLEDGEMENTS

Thank you to those in Jersey who have helped me to develop the character of Saskia Monet and her work. Thanks also to my publishers, Storm, in particular my publisher, Kathryn Taussig; editor, Natasha Hodgson; proofreader, Nicky Lovick; cover designer, Eileen Carey; and all the amazing support staff.

Finally, thanks to my family and friends for their continued support of my writing and of course to Molly dog for her patience when having to wait for walkies.

Printed in Great Britain
by Amazon